"In John Carenen's taut and exquisitely paced novel, *Keeping to Himself*, Whit Coombs' self-imposed isolation is quickly and violently interrupted one dark night beneath flashes of white-hot lightning, 'as if God were taking crime scene photos.' A powerful tale of revenge and redemption soon emerges, unfurling effortlessly like a spring thunderstorm through the coves and hollows of the book's setting in the Blue Ridge Mountains. From prologue to epilogue, Carenen's deft touch with the nuances of character and the specificity of place blanket his prose with a rare and wonderful honesty. *Keeping to Himself* is a worthy addition to the very best of Appalachian noir, but make no mistake: this is also a story of love, a story of salvation. And ultimately, Carenen's novel is about revelation . . . about discovering that true healing might arrive when you least expect it."

—Scott Gould
Author of *Whereabouts* and *Things That Crash, Things That Fly*

"Author John Carenen has crafted a single-sitting gem with *Keeping to Himself*. It is a thriller of exceptional depth and insight; a tale of murder and revenge, hard promises and regrets, secrets and the reckonings they provoke. The prose is both lean and lyrical, polished and descriptive, capturing every nuance of the verdant, simmering Southern setting and its inhabitants. It is a quick, though immersive, read, and equally indelible. I thoroughly enjoyed this book, and highly recommend it.
In fact, I might just sit back down and read it one more time."

—Baron R. Birtcher
Bestselling author of *Fistful of Rain*

"As with all of John Carenen's stories, *Keeping to Himself* is rich with description, character development, and scene setting. You will love Carenen's hero, a classic loner reminiscent of characters in David Morrell, Robert Ludlum, and John Le Carre novels. Highly recommended!"

—Joseph Badal
Award-winning author of *The Carnevale Conspiracy*

"What makes John Carenen's new novel so compelling is the central character, Whit Coombs. Coombs is a man battered by the world, yet his essential decency (as much as he wishes otherwise) will not allow him to accept an evil act, leading him and the reader into a place fraught with danger but one also offering the possibility of a new and better life."

—Ron Rash
Author of NY Times bestseller *Serena*

"John Carenen is a gifted storyteller, and *Keeping to Himself* is a high-octane blend of suspense, romance, and more than a little humor. I only wish it were longer. Don't keep this one to yourself!"

—Contributor to *From Sea to Stormy Sea, At Home in the Dark*, and *The Darkling Halls of Ivy*

"Powerful. Like the hauntingly beautiful Blue Ridge Mountains Whit Coombs calls home, the characters in *Keeping to Himself* will live with you long after you finish the last page. Carenen has done it again."

—Wendy Tyson
Author of the Amazon bestselling Greenhouse Mystery Series

Keeping to Himself

By John Carenen

Published by

3705 Shore Drive
Virginia Beach, VA 23455
800–435–4811
www.koehlerbooks.com

For Lisa (Elisabeth), my long-suffering wife, steadfast, true, and quite lovely as well. Without her encouragement, *Keeping to Himself* would have never come to be. And that's a fact. Dear bride, thank you for your love and patience.

Keeping to Himself

JOHN CARENEN

VIRGINIA BEACH
CAPE CHARLES

PROLOGUE

THE MOUNTAINS OF WESTERN North Carolina come in rows, one ridge after another. Sometimes the careful observer can see eight ridges stretching to the horizon, each a different shade of blue. They are the Appalachian Mountains, but in western North Carolina they are called the Blue Ridge.

These peaks have an abundance of vigorous streams so cold they can take your breath away if you slip in for a dip, even in August. Plunging waterfalls and turbulent rapids fling up rainbows of spray when the sun's just right. There are deep pools where trout lurk and live, and where cougar, bear, and deer come to drink. And the pristine mountain lakes lure an array of waterfowl.

The string of summits themselves are well named, one ridge giving way to another, one shade of blue to another, from azure to zaffer, stretching far into the distance. Sometimes there is just one mountain, old, worn down, and softened. And yet there are others over a mile high. The mountains are lovely, deep, and quiet. Breathtaking, one might say.

In the springtime, blossoms and wildflowers burst forth on the mountainsides, along the waterways and beside the footpaths. Dogwood, azalea, and rhododendron emerge from the branches of trees and bushes, while daffodils, pink lady slippers, and delicate, purple-painted trillium adorn the ground. Robust yellow tickseed and soft-whiskered, lavendar phalecia in abundance blanket mountain meadows.

The springtime blossoms and flowers linger through the summer, finally giving way to autumn and transforming her deciduous trees from green to fire. The mountains turn scarlet and orange, yellow and brown. And then the leaves fall and the skeletons of the trees can be seen, best against fiery sunsets as winter sets in. Often there is deep snowfall at the higher elevations, and sometimes more than a dusting drifts into the lower villages and small towns like Black Mountain, Highlands, and Saluda.

The Blue Ridge Mountains are beautiful, for sure, but not everything in them is lovely. There is danger in the hollers and ridges, and not just from fang and claw. Trouble can be found whether one is looking for it or not. The mountains, and those who dwell there, can take one's breath away. Yes, the mountains are captivating, but that doesn't mean they are safe.

CHAPTER 1

*"Trust me, there are things in this mountain that will
make your jaw bounce off the floor."*
—Jaleigh Johnson, *The Secrets of Solace*

WHIT COOMBS DIDN'T LIKE to meet people. He didn't like stiff
introductions leading to shallow small talk, being averse to such social
niceties. He possessed the skills to engage and charm, but refused to
engage or charm anymore. He'd left that behind.

"Nice to meet you, Whit," they'd say; then, "So what do you do?"

"I keep to myself," he'd reply.

A brief, awkward pause. Then, "So, are you from around here, Whit?"

"I am now."

And then there would be dead air and dropped eye contact, and the
new person would kind of sidle off after saying, "Well, good to meet you,
Whit. Have a nice day."

"You, too."

So he avoided such situations whenever he could. But if he couldn't
avoid them, like when he drove into Hastings Corners to gas up his pickup

truck, or proceeded farther down the road to Woodrow to buy supplies, or even Mitchum where the big-box stores loomed and flourished, he reluctantly acquiesced to the pressures of being polite when meeting someone he didn't want to meet. He wasn't rude.

He would shake hands and offer a fleeting smile while glancing around for something to divert the attention from him. There was always the weather. And sometimes a stray cat.

Women's social graces were more painful. They'd ask him where his wife was, although he did not wear a wedding ring, or where he worshiped. If it was the first question, he'd say she hadn't found him yet, eliciting quick smiles from the women who asked the question. If they wanted to know where he worshiped (a required question in the South), he'd just shrug and say, "Wherever the good Lord leads me."

Which was true.

The men would drift away to some vague meeting or appointment or errand. The women clung to him with more questions, especially when they discerned that he was single and reasonably handsome in a regular way. He still had all his longish black hair with just a few silver streaks, although he was pushing fifty. He wore rimless glasses and was free of tattoos.

One woman, probably a poet, said he had a "handsome, damaged face," and he guessed she was maybe right, accounting for some women's taste in men. His right ear was misshapen from wrestling in high school; scar tissue around his eyebrows spoke to a few years in the Army; and his broken nose, still a little crooked from a fight a few months previous, gave a kind of rugged character to his countenance.

But this was a good spring morning, he thought as he filled up his old Ford F-150 at Homer's Gas & Groceries in Hastings Corners. He'd rolled down the windows before they left home, and now his boulder-big dog, Barney, a short-haired mixed breed with some Bullmastiff or Cane Corso antecedents, sat obediently in the front seat as Whit pumped gas. He screwed the gas cap tight, then filled up two portable five-gallon containers for use around the cabin and, one in each hand, set them in the back of the truck, secured with a bungee cord.

Whit had found Barney as a scrawny puppy, half frozen and trapped in a snowbank on the side of the road partway up the mountain one night three winters ago. The dark brindle and white-splotched puppy had been abandoned and left to freeze to death. Whit stopped his truck, grabbed his snow shovel from the truck bed, and dug the dog out, knocking away clumps of ice stuck to the freezing animal's hindquarters.

Then he carried the dog home and thawed him out. The next day he took Barney in to see Henry Moreland, the local vet, who said the pup was healthy except for worms. Pills took care of that. Quality dog food and love ushered Barney into what he was now—an affable giant who loved people, despite his earlier mistreatment. Barney slept next to Whit's feet at night, typically taking more than his share of the bed.

Whit eased up to the cash register in the store, picked out three packages of Zingers (the kind with the yellow frosting), two for himself and one for Barney, and pulled out his wallet and waited for Homer to finish restocking his beer cooler.

"That fucking dog's as ugly as your fucking truck."

Whit looked behind him. It was J. D. "Hacker" Merrone, local tough guy, a big man always getting on Whit's case, wanting a fight. Hacker's shadow and partner in ennui, Buford Butz, half the size of Hacker, nodded and grinned, his meth-decimated teeth dominating his pockmarked, skeletal face.

Whit looked back at the Zingers in front of him on the counter and said nothing. "You know that dog's mine," Hacker continued, his high-pitched voice belying his significant size. "He slipped away from me that night and ran off. Reckon I could just go ahead and take him. Reckon I'll just go ahead and do that now."

Whit turned and watched the two men leave the store. Homer finished with the cooler and eased his bulk behind the counter. Whit told him how much gas he'd pumped, pushed the three Zingers forward, and opened his wallet.

"Anything else I can do ya for, Whit?"

Whit shook his head. Homer totaled up the bill, and Whit paid. While he was jamming his wallet back in his hip pocket and gathering up his change, he heard an explosion of sound from outside the store—a man shrieking in a falsetto inspired by terror. Whit spotted Hacker leaning against the passenger-side door of the pickup truck, squirming a little. Buford Butz danced around him, tugging at his pal without success.

"Uh-oh," Whit said softly, then scooped up the junk food triumphs and walked outside, Homer and two customers following to see what the trouble was.

"Get this fucking dog off me!" Hacker shouted, his right arm and shoulder inside the truck through the partly-open door. Whit strolled up and peered inside. Barney had the man's shoulder in his mouth. Without releasing Hacker, the big dog looked into his master's eyes and wagged his tail.

Whit said, "Okay, Barney," and the dog let go of the man, who quickly moved away, rubbing his shoulder. There were no puncture holes in Hacker Merrone's camo T-shirt. Just a bit of slobber.

"I'm going to sue your ass and have this monster put down!" Hacker said.

Barney growled and continued to wag his big tail.

Homer laughed and said, "So you tell the judge your arm was inside Whit's truck because . . . ?"

"Fuck you, Homer," Buford said. And the two men stalked off, muttering curses.

"Didn't even leave a mark," Homer said, laughing and shaking his head. The two other bystanders shuffled back inside the store.

Whit circled around to the driver's side, got in, and drove away, unwrapping Barney's Zinger as he went.

Back inside the store, Homer laughed with the other two bystanders and said, "Gotta admire Whit's restraint. Somebody mess with my dog, I'd slap that boy upside the head."

"Maybe so," one of the men replied, "but then you know Hacker would get back at you some sneaky-ass way. Man's a menace."

"You can say that again," said the other man as he watched Merrone and Butz walk away.

The first man picked up a bag of Cheetos. "No need to."

CHAPTER 2

"Bad people are intriguing."
—Jorge Garcia

THE LOCAL BAR, On Second Thought, was open across the street from Homer's Gas & Grocery, and its capability to offer liquid remedies for pain beckoned Hacker and Buford. Leaving their pickup truck at Homer's, they crossed the street in the late-morning sunshine. They passed through the parking lot, skirting a moped and a banged-up El Camino with mismatched doors, climbed the three front steps, and pushed inside.

"Ow!" Buford said as Hacker entered the bar and let the door slam back on his friend. "That hurts, dude!"

"I'm the one what's hurtin'," Hacker said, rubbing his right shoulder. "Fuckin' dog needs to be put down."

"Yeah, like that's gonna happen," Buford said.

Two older, bearded men were seated at a booth against the wall, nursing beers and pale, unidentifiable food on their plates. They looked up, looked away. At a table, another man, not much more than a boy, sat drinking a clear liquid from a Mason jar with a handle. He did not acknowledge the new patrons.

The two men moseyed across the sticky floor and up to the bar. A tall, fat man wearing a gray T-shirt with *Naughty girl! Go to my room!* written across his sagging chest said, "Hacker. Buford. What'll it be this mornin', boys?"

"Shots and PBR, Sterling," Hacker said.

"For both of you?"

Hacker looked at Buford, who nodded.

"A little early for that, ain't it?" the bartender asked.

"Just do it. Whatcha got to eat?" Buford asked.

"Tex-Mex stuff from the microwave. Sandwiches from the fridge. Grill ain't up yet."

"Gimme a coupla enchiladas," Hacker said.

"Me too," Buford said.

"I saw your little set-to with that man's dog," Sterling said. He chuckled.

"You know I can break your head," Hacker said.

"Reckon so," Sterling said, "but you're welcome to try me sometime."

"Hacker'd take you easy, man," Buford snapped.

"Looked like that was a big dog what bit you," the bartender said, ignoring Buford. "Let's see it." He nodded toward Hacker's shoulder.

Hacker glared.

Sterling shrugged, smiled, and poured them both a shot glass of whiskey and fetched two cans of Pabst Blue Ribbon from the cooler under the counter. He popped the caps and slid the cold cans across the bar. The two men took their drinks to a table in the back under the mounted head of a four-point buck missing a glass eye.

"We're hungry, so step on the food!" Buford hollered over his shoulder.

"Sounds messy," Sterling said as he set to the food orders.

Merrone and Butz pulled out chairs from the stained formica table and sat. They tossed back their shots and followed up with long pulls of beer. Nothing was said for a moment.

"Keep the shots comin'," Hacker called to the bar. Sterling nodded, fetched a bottle from behind the bar on his way to their table, poured two more shots and left.

The men sucked in the whiskey and sipped their beers.

"We gotta figure out some way to fuck up Coombs. He's been messin' with me long enough," Hacker said.

"What about?" Buford asked, taking another swig of beer.

"That goddamn dog, for one thing. And that time at the Walmart."

"But that ain't true about him bein' your dog."

"Buford, would you just shut up? I know that, but that's just an example. He shoulda just let me have that dog when I claimed it. Shoulda let me take it with me just now 'stead of settin' it on me."

"He didn't set it on you. You reached in to get him."

With surprising quickness for a man his size, Hacker slapped Buford's head. "Look, numbnuts, Coombs messed with me, and he did it with people watchin'. Worse, he ignored me, like I was nothin' but white trash. Yeah, I'm gonna put a hurtin' on Whit Coombs. You can bet on it."

Buford rubbed the back of his head, a hurt expression on his face. A microwave dinged over by the bar, and shortly, Sterling brought over two paper plates with enchiladas on them, and two cellophane packs of plastic cutlery. He held out the whiskey bottle he'd carried against his side, raised his eyebrows in invitation. Hacker shook his head and the big bartender left.

Hacker muttered, "Oughta put Coombs down and take the dog."

"That monster'd make us some serious cash in the ring."

"Got that right," Hacker said.

CHAPTER 3

"Mist around a mountain; all reality is there."
—Marty Rubin

WHIT'S CABIN STOOD THREE MILES down an unnamed dirt lane that broke off from Screaming Panther Road, a crumbling blacktop eyesore in need of maintenance. A spine of weeds and grass split the trail in the middle as it disappeared around a corner into a copse of trees, mostly ancient loblolly pines stretching over one hundred feet in the air. The route wound through thicker stands of other, leafy trees and deep shadows until it came to an abrupt end at a small, graveled parking area bordered by railroad ties on three sides. A few yards beyond that stood the cabin.

The structure itself was over 150 years old when Whit purchased it. Comprised of thick logs, cedar shakes, and a stone fireplace, the place had good bones but suffered from neglect. No one had lived there for years. It had been abandoned, like a classic car on cinder blocks, waiting for restoration.

Realtors talked too much and tended to hyperbole, flaws Whit found annoying, so on his own he had searched in two or three counties he liked, looking for a home. He drove down country roads, up shadowy private lanes, seeking *For Sale* signs. On occasion, he would approach a home he liked, even if it wasn't for sale, and offer the owner a chance to sell. That never worked, and now and then he was met with hostility.

One late afternoon after another fruitless foray, Whit gave up and dropped by On Second Thought, that gritty pub which catered to failures, those determined to fail but not yet entirely successful, and retired substitute mail carriers. Whit, a poor fit for any of the categories, stopped by for liquid comfort, fueled by a mild curiosity about the bar he had never patronized. He did not like bars in general—too noisy, bad smells, and the potential for fisticuffs.

Whit took a stool at the bar and ordered a Sam Adams Boston Lager. He asked the barkeep if there was property for sale nearby, and provided a general description of what he wanted. The bartender, built like a sumo wrestler, nodded in the direction of a bulletin board where Whit found posted notices for septic tank pumping, free kittens to a good home, and three taxidermists—and a smudged three-by-five card advertising a cabin and acreage for $175,000.

Whit returned to the bar. "How long's the ad been posted?"

"Year, year and a half," the bartender said with a shrug, turning to another patron.

Whit nodded, walked back over to the notice, memorized the number, and called the next morning. Directions were given by the seller and a meeting at the property arranged. Whit arrived early and drove down the dirt road. The cabin stood in a sunny clearing, surrounded by forest and mountains. A creek fed into a large, blue lake twenty yards behind the structure. The day spoke of spring, a chill in the air, drifting mist on the mountains obscuring their peaks. Whit stifled his reaction to the property, afraid to hope, a word that had mostly slipped away from him over the years.

He moseyed around to the front of the cabin when he heard a vehicle approaching. A black Cadillac Escalade emerged from the spring-greening maple, sugar maple, and yellow poplars bordering the lane and came to a stop. Eventually, the driver's door opened and a man well into the winter of his years emerged wearing a black turtleneck sweater, black jeans, cowboy boots, and a gray wool winter coat. A Greek fisherman's cap perched on his head, and little, white, wispy curls squeezed out from under it.

The man approached Whit with careful steps, as if his feet were brittle. The men shook hands and introduced themselves and exchanged minimal small talk about the weather. Then Whit got down to business.

"How many acres?" he asked. "You said an acreage."

"Fifty-three, more or less," the man said. He bent a little to one side but carried himself as someone of means. "Course, it's smack against the Nantahala National Forest, so you don't have to worry about neighbors." It was more land than Whit had guessed.

"So why are you selling it?" Whit asked.

The old man smiled a rueful smile and said, "History of sadness. A lot of lonesome out here."

A good match for me, Whit thought. "It's a fair price," he said.

"It's a steal."

"I'll pay what you're asking."

"Don't you want to look inside?"

"I looked through the windows. I walked around out back."

"You saw the deck and dock."

"Yes."

"Any questions?" the man asked.

"None."

The two men shook hands again. Five minutes had passed.

And that was that. Three days later, Whit Coombs owned the place. That was nearly four years ago.

He fixed it up, called Duke Power to repair the line snapped by a branch from a dead pin oak tree. Once the line was restored to the main source along Panther Scream Road, there was electricity to get him started. It took two months of satisfying hard work. Whit lost six pounds and gained callouses, muscle, and a bit of sun on his face and arms. He stocked the kitchen and pantry. He bought a red cedar canoe and two paddles encapsulated in fiberglass. He was satisfied. Good house, good land. Privacy.

Whit fell deliberately into comfortable routines. First thing in the morning, he would drop down to his knees beside his bed and pray, "Lord Jesus, forgive me, a miserable sinner"—and mean it. He did not enumerate specific sins. The good Lord knew, and that took care of his daily relationship with the Almighty, a theology not easily contradicted, and one that gave him comfort and humility.

Then he would climb to his feet, order Barney off the bed, and wait for the big dog with the intelligent brown eyes to regretfully slide down like a slow-motion avalanche. Whit would make the bed, hospital corners and all. He was grateful that Barney never refused the "get down" order because there was no moving Barney if he didn't want to move.

Whit would then dress and start the coffee maker. While coffee was brewing, he let the big dog outside and made his own breakfast, filled up Barney's food and water dishes, and considered the day before him. Then he would call in the dog and they would have breakfast together. Sometimes chores needed his attention, other times a book would call his name, and on occasion he took a trip into town or just went for a drive for the fun of it.

Going out on an exploration with Barney was always a pleasure. The two of them inevitably found something worthwhile: a new ice cream stand, a trout stream to wade in, or a nature trail that beckoned. A better barbecue joint. They would be gone all day and return to their place tired and happy to see their home waiting for them in the clearing in the deep mountain woods.

Whit loved the mountains, much as others from flat places loved the peaks more than the natives born and raised in the highlands who took the natural beauty around them for granted. Sometimes Whit had to pinch himself to accept how good his life was. He was strong and healthy, he lived in a beautiful setting, and he had a good dog. No financial worries or need to get a job. The lump-sum payment from the VA, together with most of his savings, had allowed Whit to buy the property outright. His Army disability check was more than adequate to live on since he had no debt. And in a few years he'd be old enough to also draw Social Security.

Whit Coombs had solitude. He had control of his life. And he was pretty much free of responsibility. The only speed bump in his smooth ride were the nightmares about her—infrequent now, but still there, deep in his mind, entrenched and ready to show up at any time.

He enjoyed being bone tired at the end of most days, and liked going to bed, Barney flopping down at the foot. Hard physical activity was cleansing, and hikes deep into the mountains had proven to be therapeutic, a kind of solitude that led to purification. Sporadic the first few months, hikes had become habitual and almost daily over the years.

Sometimes Whit hiked at night, striding mostly unarmed into the bosom of the mountains. He would leave Barney behind to avoid being distracted by the big, curious canine, who often plunged into the darkness, inspired by a strange and exciting sniff. At night there was less to see and more to hear, if one was not afraid to listen.

CHAPTER 4

*"That night there was more than one killer
in the forest, the next day a lot more ghosts."*
—Michale J. Sullivan, *Age of Myth*

NO ONE REALLY KNEW Whit Coombs. That was one reason he moved from Hendersonville into the mountains. Oh, there were people who saw him, people who spoke with him, others who only recognized him. But no one knew him. There was power in anonymity. No expectations of him, accountable only to himself—and Barney.

Some who interacted with him on his forays into Hastings Corner or Woodrow felt sorry for him when they eventually learned that he lived deep in the hollers with that big dog, all alone. They pitied him. Others said he was just a misanthrope and better left to himself. And some—men who married too young out of boredom and lived in sullen acceptance of disappointing lives—envied him, and wished to be like that strange fella with the big dog. But on this particular night, being like Whit Coombs would be the last thing they'd want.

His day had been good, and so he took a nap in the middle of the afternoon, resting up for a night hike. He knew the lay of the land after all these years, memorizing not only the footpaths of people but also the more obscure paths made by animals, mostly deer, through the mountainous forest by way of rugged heights and along rocky precipices.

Whit was sure-footed and strong and smart, with excellent hearing in one ear and glasses to sharpen his sight, and he enjoyed feeling at home any time of the day or night in the ruggedness of the Nantahala National Forest that bordered his land. And night hiking was special, private, with no chance of bumping into the stray hiker or group of curious Scouts.

It was nearly eleven when he laced up his hiking boots and started for the door, telling Barney he'd be back later. The big dog looked disappointed at being left behind, but Whit knew his buddy would soon be on the sofa by the door, snoring away, waiting for his return. It was nice to be missed, and nice to be welcomed back every time.

The early-summer night was clear, plenty of starlight and a gibbous moon offering up more illumination than Whit needed, although he welcomed it. He took very little with him—just his Swiss Army knife. He did not own a cell phone, or a landline for that matter, and he did not take his handgun or a flashlight as he had when he was not as knowledgeable about the terrain.

Whit believed if he ran into trouble, he'd be able to handle it. The slight possibility of danger or an accident added a little excitement to his hikes, especially at night. But he knew he wouldn't see anyone. On day hikes, because of people, he carried his handgun, his knife, a couple of energy bars, and a canteen. Tonight, he carried only the knife.

The sky clouded up about an hour into his hike to the bridge at Byers' Creek, followed by a strong breeze. Whit knew a storm was coming. He rarely looked at weather reports. He couldn't do anything about the weather except adjust to it.

The rain started a little later, first as a soft mist that swayed and drifted through the trees like a lacey curtain, then strengthening into strong and steady rain, and finally filling out as a full-fledged downpour pounding and blowing in stiff sheets across the rocky face of the mountain. Brilliant bolts of lightning stabbed here and there, occasionally cracking into trees and splitting them open, leaving the acrid smell of ozone in the air. Whit startled with each clap.

He hiked a good distance while it rained, thinking about turning around. But he was already soaked, and his goal had been to reach the simple bridge still ahead, a narrow construction without guardrails, a dirt road on each side.

Whit had never seen a car or truck on the bridge. Until tonight.

But there it was when Whit arrived about eighty yards downstream: a battered old pickup parked in the middle of the bridge. Lightning strikes flashed on the wet, tossing leaves, and slender branches whipped around by the windstorm as if they were waving and warning him away, followed by abrupt, enormous peals of thunder for emphasis.

Whit crouched behind a bush, taking off his glasses to run his thumb across the wet lenses and put them back on. He made out three figures. Two were tormenting the third, whose hands appeared to be pinned behind him. One of the two men looked familiar, but at that distance, Whit could not see well enough to identify him. The other, much smaller, continued to punch and kick and slap the helpless third man.

Another strobe of lightning reflected on metal in the big man's hand, a knife being drawn across the forehead of the captive, whose mouth opened wide in a scream that Whit heard despite the storm. The man's mouth was a black hole, a tight rictus of pain and despair as he slumped in the grip of the smaller man, his face covered in blood.

Thunder shook the mountain, followed by a dying wind and eerie silence as the rumbles rolled east. Whit crouched, stunned, fearful, angry. Then he heard a high, squeaky voice from the big man. "Last chance, man. Where the fuck is it, Tory!"

Tory wept and screamed, "But I don't *know!*"

Whit watched in horror as the big man plunged the knife over and over again into Tory, who wailed his fear and despair with each stab of the blade. The big man paused a second and wiped his hand on his mouth. Then, in one final motion, he drew the steel across the victim's throat, the macabre scene lit by another flare, as if God were taking crime scene photos.

The smaller man held Tory up for a moment as he bled to death, and then let him slump, lifeless, to the ground. Lightning again cracked through the black night, giving Whit a better look at the two men, who glanced around and in his direction, then back down at their victim. The retreating thunder sounded through the mountains like a giant's fleeing footfalls.

The big man bent down and grabbed the corpse under the arms as the other man tucked a handgun into his belt and hefted the legs. One, two, and on the third swing they slung Tory over the side of the small bridge and into the rocky stream where he flopped, drifted a few yards, and became wedged between a pair of boulders.

The men cursed and laughed and climbed into the truck. Flipping on the headlights, they headed on across the bridge and up a muddy dirt road angled along the mountainside.

Whit stood, drenched, his T-shirt and jeans heavy and cold. He briefly thought about clambering down to look at the body. No use. Would he call the cops and tell them what he saw? Not likely. If he did that, if he called the law, he would be drawn into a situation that was none of his business.

Still, he was troubled by the one thing he knew. The big man with the squeaky voice was Hacker Merrone, and his buddy had to be Buford Butz.

CHAPTER 5

"I've never met a murderer who wasn't vain. . . .
They may be frightened of getting caught, but they
can't help strutting and boasting and usually
they're sure they've been far too clever to be caught."
—Agatha Christie, *Crooked House*

HACKER MERRONE CURSED EVERYTHING he could think of—the weather, the dead Tory Cook, Buford Butz, and God—and then cursed everything again.

"What you cussin' me for?" Buford whined.

"Because you're a dipshit. Because you don't know nothin'. Because you're *you*, Buford."

"I didn't do nothin' t' be cussed. Jesus, Hacker, I'm jus' tryin' to be helpful."

"You're useless as tits on a bull, Buford. I shoulda cut *your* throat."

The truck careened and slid on the narrow, muddy road, headlights whipping into trees and rock overhangs and bouncing off the pouring rain. Twice, the vehicle nearly slid off the face of the mountain, but Hacker guided it back on course. Conversation left the truck cabin, the two men overcome by fear and frustration. Incessant, deafening rain pounded on the roof as if its fury had been inflamed by what happened back at the bridge.

The road flattened, and Merrone turned in at a wide spot backed up to a sagging, rust-streaked mobile home. He braked to a stop in the weed-choked yard, headlights on the ramshackle rectangle. Buford had just opened his door when Merrone grabbed him by the neck and jerked him back.

"Burn those clothes you're wearin', Buford. I mean it. And do it tonight. I'm doing mine, and I'm gonna get rid of my knife and then wipe down the inside of this truck with bleach."

"What?"

"Do like I told you. Don't need no evidence around of what we done. I'm ditchin' the knife where no one will find it. After I wipe it down."

"Okay, Hacker. Will do," Butz muttered. He slid out of the truck, slammed the door shut, and trudged toward his trailer, his mind churning over Hacker's words. *"What we done." Ain't no "we" in this*, Buford thought. *Hacker did the killin'.* Butz slipped inside his home, and the truck's lights went away.

He headed for his refrigerator and took out three beers still looped together. Buford was crying. What Hacker had done was a whole lot more serious than pissing in public, or even roughing up some tootsie in a bar if she resisted his pawings. *God Almighty!* He opened the first beer and collapsed on a sagging sofa.

Hacker muttered out loud on his way farther up the mountain to his home. "Dumbass didn't realize we weren't funnin' him. All he had to do was tell us where he'd hid that two grand and we would've let him go. Maybe even give him a ride home. Course, he'd have to ride in the back in the rain, but least he'd be alive."

Merrone went silent and concentrated on keeping the truck on the road. A couple of miles later, he pulled up the gravel driveway that led to his mother's house—a small, brick, ranch-style home with rose bushes in the front yard.

The kennel dogs erupted into snarls and barks as Hacker stopped the truck and got out. "SHUT UP!" he shouted, and except for a couple of whimpers, silence followed. The front door opened, a big body screening off most of the light from inside as Merrone approached the house.

Her white hair pulled back in a severe bun, the woman crossed thick arms, propping up her ponderous breasts. "You got the fuckin' money, son?"

"No," Merrone said, pushing past his mother and into the house.

"So, what the hell did you *do*? Just tell Tory it was okay and maybe kiss him on his cheek? Tell him not to do that shit no more? Give him a break?" She slapped her son's face as he brushed by.

"Me and Buford took care of him," Merrone said, rubbing his cheek. He strode over to the kitchen counter that divided the rooms and picked up an uncapped Mason jar with clear liquid inside. He drank, swallowed, shuddered, and drank some more. Then he wiped his mouth.

"Son, I don't want you drinkin' from the jar. That's nasty. Get a glass. Come talk to me," she said, plopping down into an overstuffed chair. "Now tell me. What the hell happened? And don't leave nothin' out, boy, 'cause I can smell blood on you."

The son supplied his mother with abundant details as if he were reading a grocery list.

"Anybody see you? Any chance?" she asked, leaning forward in her chair.

"Are you shittin' me? Middle of the night, big storm, way up on Byers' Creek bridge? Ain't nobody that crazy. No, ma'am, no witnesses. Jesus!"

"I was wonderin' about that man does all the hikin' up 'round there. Strange fella bought the Henningson place a while back. You know Rita Runnels lives way back in there, she says he's up there all'a time, sometimes with a big dog. Day and night. Odd fella. No chance he saw you?"

"That's Whit Coombs, and hell no, he weren't up there. I looked around."

"Good idea to find out for sure," she said, settling back. "You leave any traces? Anything that could connect you to the body?"

"Not a thing. I told Buford to burn his clothes. I'll get rid of my knife in the morning. I'll wipe it down before I bury it. And I'll get the truck wiped down with bleach come first light."

"No fuckin' 'first light,' boy! You do it right now and do it right. And don't tell me where you bury the knife, neither! Gives me that 'pausible deniability' they talk about on TV. Now get goin'! NOW!"

Merrone, who had yet to sit down, defiantly took another drink from the jar, said nothing, and set to his orders.

When the door slammed shut, Angie Merrone shook her head. *Shit! That miscarriage I had was smarter than this one. Two thousand bucks, he kills a man. Now we'll never get it back. Dumb as a post, that one. We'll be alright, though. No one will miss Tory Cook. The mountains can keep a secret.*

She got up with a grunt after rocking back and forth twice, and headed for the kitchen. There she retrieved a big glass tumbler from an overhead cabinet, and put together her favorite beverage for "nerves"— Diet Dr. Pepper half and half with Knob Creek Straight Kentucky Bourbon Whiskey.

She sucked in a couple of steady glugs, and the soothing heat and sweetness suffused her body like a prayer of gratitude. A few minutes later, Hacker came in the back door stark naked and wet.

"I done what you told me, Ma," he said.

"Come in here, son. I got a thought," she said, stretching her wide legs out in front of her. "Might be about right for you."

"Just a minute while I put on somethin' dry," he said.

She heard him open the clothes dryer on the back porch, then grunting as he dressed. He came into the living room. "What is it?"

"Sit down, JD."

He sat, resting his brawny forearms on his thighs.

"You know what you need? Something to settle you down. Maybe cut down on your running with Butz and those other boys, what's their names—those Davis boys."

"Mikey and Slug."

"And that other one, with the straying eye."

"Ray Thornton."

"Whatever, you need to settle down. Get a woman and marry her. Gimme a grandbaby or two. You get some of that honeypot reg'lar, and that would fix it."

"I don't need no wife to get some of that sweetness," Hacker sighed. "Jesus, Mom. I ain't about to pay for it or get married for it. I get what I need."

"Yeah, and I know how you do it. Grabbin' and slappin' around until you're done is gonna get you in trouble."

"Not if they keep their pretty mouths shut. Not if I can remind them that life is too sweet to have it taken away," he said.

"Too bad Tory couldn't be convinced about that," she laughed. Hacker laughed with her.

He said, "So, anyways, no need to get married. Besides, look at me, Mom. Fat and ugly. Who'd want me?"

"Take after yo' daddy."

"Whoever he was," Hacker said.

Angie Merrone gave her son the finger.

CHAPTER 6

"The mountains themselves call us into greater stories."
—Donald Miller

WHILE MERRONE AND BUTZ worked their way higher up the mountain, Whit stumbled and slipped down the muddy footpath, thinking of what he just witnessed. Halfway home, a scream nearly separated his mind from his body.

It sounded like a terrified woman being tortured, or gazing upon something so vile and vicious and demonic that all she could do was wail from the core of her being. And then the guttural, blood-chilling shrieking came again, speaking of agony and despair and mind-numbing pain. And it came again, a third time, and then no more. No sound but the light rain patting down on the leaves of the trees as the storm eased.

Whit stood rooted to the trail. The cry had sounded nearby, and behind him. But he knew the woods and rocks could play tricks with sound, so he was not sure of the woman's location. He didn't know what to do, but he had to do something. He took a half dozen tentative steps.

Then a realization settled his scattered spirit. He lived just off Panther

Scream Road, didn't he? Hadn't he heard the stories of how the road got its name, that it wound through panther country, where the screams of a woman in travail could sometimes be heard? Twice over the years he had seen a black panther. In the early-morning mist it had emerged like a liquid shadow from the tree line of his property and slipped down to the small lake for a drink. This could be the same animal.

But a panther was out there, for sure, behind him. He picked up his pace as much as the obscure, narrow path would allow and made good time back to his cabin with no further screams to unsettle him. There was already enough to unsettle him without that intrusion.

Safe inside and greeted by Barney, Whit turned on lights, showered, dressed in clean clothes, and started a load of laundry that included his wet things. He grabbed a bottle of Jim Beam and poured three fingers in a glass and sat down—to sort through what he had seen, and reconsider what he should have done instead of what he actually did.

Was there anything he could have done to stop the slaughter of this Tory person? No, he was too far away without his handgun, and the attack was already ending. Should he have confronted the killers? Under the circumstances, Whit pondered how that would have benefitted anyone. Would they have thanked him for his intervention and repented? More likely they would have immediately taken action to get rid of a witness; after all, they had a gun, and he was unarmed except for his little knife.

As a witness, then, what should he do now? *Ah*, Whit thought, *there's the rub*. Call the cops? He didn't know anything about the Ransom County sheriff, didn't even know who he was. Whit wondered what would he say. "I saw Hacker Merrone and Buford Butz kill a man up on the Byers' Creek bridge"? What then? Would he go with the county sheriff to search the crime scene and find the body? The men had not taken the corpse with them, so it might still be there in the morning.

Whit finished his drink and stood, refilled his glass with three fingers more, and paced around his living room, running his hands through his hair. *Okay, suppose the sheriff arrested Merrone and Butz. Then what? A trial?*

His word against theirs. And how gifted did a defense attorney have to be to scuttle his identification of the two defendants?

"So, how is your, um, vision, Mr. Coombs? Do you wear glasses? Were you wearing your glasses that night? Wasn't it raining hard that night? On your glasses? Maybe blurring them a bit? And how far were you from the crime scene? Eighty yards? And, oh, was it dark outside that night? Weren't the moon and stars obscured by the thunderstorm taking place?"

Further, Whit realized, the defense attorney would no doubt pick at his own lifestyle and history. His "peculiar" desire to live alone in the woods, the fact that he was on disability from the Army ("And what did you *do* in the Army?"—an unanswerable question), and the defense would no doubt discover he had damaged hearing in one ear ("You say you *heard* Mr. Marrone. Which ear did you *hear* with?"). Also the fact that Whit had been in a fight a while back. They might even probe into why he had such a big dog.

No doubt Merrone and Butz would have ironclad alibis provided by friends, family, neighbors. And everybody in the mountains had a knife.

Whit finished his second whiskey, placed the glass in the sink, and rinsed it. He took out a container of pimento cheese spread ("Southern caviar") and a loaf of bread. He was hungry at last. A long walk, a traumatic crime, and being scared witless by panther screams had built up an appetite.

He slathered two slices of bread with the spread, folded them together, and ate standing up at the kitchen counter. After giving an attentive Barney the last bite, he pulled a partial half gallon of caramel swirl ice cream out of the freezer and finished its remains, tossing the carton into the trash. Barney sat patiently at his feet.

"You wanna go out?"

The big dog rose quickly and ran to the back door, turning and fixing his eyes on his master. Thinking about the panther, Whit grabbed his rifle and turned on the outdoor lights to watch from the deck as Barney took care of business. It was still raining a little, more of a sprinkle.

Whit wondered how his dog would do against coyotes or the panther, then decided Barney's sheer size would act as a deterrent to an attack. He called the big canine, and they hurried back inside together. Whit took a rough bath towel and rubbed down his companion, who then jumped onto the sofa and lay down and watched his friend.

Whit stood in the middle of the room, hands on hips, rocking back and forth on his feet. He was able to dismiss the panther scream; although a rare phenomenon, it was a natural thing for a panther to do. A biological entity driven by its biology. But he could not shake the murder of the man. He sat in his recliner.

He had seen bad things in the Army, mostly after they happened. Mass killings, victims of torture, victims of rape. But the cold, remorseless, deliberate stabbing and execution of Tory before Whit's eyes had brought a new kind of horror into his experience. He imagined what went through the man's mind as he was being stabbed, without hope of surviving, condemned to a grisly, painful death at the hands of people he knew, just because he could not tell them where something was. And what was that, by the way? A cache of drugs, a bundle of money? Something else of great value?

Whit at least felt confident he had gone unnoticed. Well hidden behind a thick bush in the dark and rain, a long way from the killing, he knew he had seen without being seen, even though Hacker had briefly glanced his way. If Hacker had seen him, Whit believed, he would have come down the faint deer trail to try to kill him, too.

Whit relaxed into his recliner, pulled the lever for the footrest, and took a deep breath. Eventually, law enforcement would sort it all out. First, someone would say that Tory was missing. That, or the body would be discovered by some solitary trout fisherman or nature walker. Either way, the professionals would then step in and conduct a thorough investigation. They would solve the crime, or they would relegate it to the cold case files—probably the latter because there were no witnesses, no confessions, and no clues. There would be solid alibis if Merrone or Butz were implicated by innuendo, reputation, or fact.

If the case went unsolved, Whit knew that eventually it would all go away. Maybe the ghost of Tory would be seen up in the hollers along the stream, just another bit of local folklore for which the mountains were well known.

Satisfied with his thinking, Whit left his recliner, stripped down to his T-shirt and boxers, turned out all the lights, and went to bed. Shortly after, Barney arranged himself with a grunt at the foot of the bed, generously allowing Whit enough room to straighten his legs. Whit relaxed into his decision to leave things alone, to keep to himself.

In a matter of minutes, there were dueling snores in the little cabin in the Blue Ridge Mountains.

CHAPTER 7

"The truth is, hardly any of us have ethical energy enough
for more than one really inflexible point of honor."
—George Bernard Shaw

IN THE MORNING, Whit stretched, rolled out of bed, and fell to his knees for his morning prayer. "Lord Jesus, forgive me, a miserable sinner."

He thought about what he had just asked. And then he simply accepted that his sincere request had been answered as he spoke it, rose, and let Barney out. He prepared coffee and breakfast and turned on the local TV station.

The morning news lady was asking viewers if they had any information on the whereabouts of one Tory Cook, thirty-five years old, Caucasion, about five foot six and 130 pounds, last seen three days ago at a McDonald's in Brevard. His photo was on the screen. Mug shot. The man's sallow complexion, acne scars, and small brown eyes spoke to misery. A number to call was displayed at the bottom of the screen. Then the reporter moved on to a story about a church that had burned down under suspicious circumstances.

The next day, Whit chopped wood to add to his woodpile in preparation for winter. It was midsummer and hot. After he mowed the yard he took his canoe out for a brief ride, gliding over the cool, glassy waters as he paddled to the center of the blue lake, watching the clear water slide down the side of the yellow paddle. He let the canoe drift as he breathed deeply and scanned the woods and the mountains beyond in their shades of blue. No other homes were visible around the lake. Except for Whit's plot, the shoreline belonged to the national forest.

That evening, Whit turned to the local news again and there it was again.

Same reporter, but with a somber face. Same photo of Tory Cook. The body had been found by a Boy Scout troop studying the quaint little bridge as a key element of their day's hike. One of the boys had looked downstream and seen a person wedged between two boulders like a pendant on a busty woman.

Again, the news lady reached out to her audience, asking if anyone knew anything about the "suspicious death" of Tory Cook and to please call the Ransom County Sheriff's Department at the number on the bottom of the screen.

Whit figured someone would make the call, and the wobbly wheels of justice would grind out an outcome acceptable to the citizenry, with Hacker and Buford being brought to justice. Or not. Whit did not make the call. None of his business.

A day later, his chores were interrupted by the sound of a car creeping down his twisting driveway. He walked out to the gravel parking area and waited. The white car had a light bar across the roof and a woman behind the wheel. When it pulled in and stopped, he saw the green Ransom County Sheriff's Department insignia on the passenger door. The driver got out and strode up to him, removing her big sunglasses.

About five foot four with short blonde hair, the woman looked fit. Her tan uniform—tailored, starched, creased—pulled a little tightly across the chest. The top button of the blouse was unbuttoned, a white T-shirt underneath. She wore mid-thigh shorts that revealed tan, muscular legs.

Her equipment belt included what looked like a Glock 9. The name tag on her chest read *Della Render* and *Ransom County Sheriff.* Late-forties. Whit decided to be wise in how he addressed the woman—to acknowledge her position and mute his surprise.

"Sheriff Render. What can I do for you?" he asked, turning his good, left ear to her voice.

"You Whit Coombs, sir?" Her voice sounded soft.

"I am."

"I believe you might have heard about a suspicious death up north of here a few miles? Man named Tory Cook." She hung her sunglasses on the T-shirt collar, revealing large, gray eyes. *Beautiful,* he thought, *and intelligent, curious. A little pushy.*

"Saw it on the news." Whit removed his rimless glasses, held them up to the light, put them back on.

"I was wondering if you knew anything about it. I've heard that you are a man familiar with the woods and the mountains, a man who hikes nearly every day, or *night*, and has for years. Is that so?"

"It is."

She studied his face in the quiet midmorning. Whit noticed small beads of perspiration along the sheriff's upper lip and forehead. He wanted to touch the sweat away. His thermometer outside the kitchen window registered ninety-four degrees at 10 AM, half an hour ago. Hotter now. He was suddenly aware that he was wearing a sweaty T-shirt along with his cutoffs and work boots. He took a chance.

"More questions? Cooler inside." *Why did I say that?*

Sheriff Render's face opened up from serious to a big smile, white teeth made whiter in contrast to her suntan. "Thank you," she said.

"This way," Whit said, and immediately felt stupid. *Of course it's this way. We're here and the cabin is there.*

Inside, Barney slithered sleepily off one of the sofas and trotted up to her, tail wagging. She reached her left hand out, a fist with the palm down so he could sniff. He licked her hand and she stroked his domed head.

"This is a magnificent dog, Mr. Coombs," she said. "What's his name?"

"Barney."

She smiled. "Fits," she said. "He's a big boy. How much does he weigh?"

"About 130 pounds."

"Purebred?"

"No. Mutt. Mostly Bullmastiff, and maybe some Cane Corso mixed in. Not sure. Would you like some sweet tea?" he asked. *Dumb! Don't encourage her to stay around.*

She said, "Thank you. Never heard of Cane Corso."

"Big breed," he said, thinking, *There you go being dumb again—master of the obvious comment.*

"I guess so."

He fetched sweet tea for both of them, gave her a glass and kept the other. They sat facing each other over the low coffee table.

"Mr. Coombs, how long have you lived here? I didn't even know there was a cabin down this path, and I've been sheriff for six years."

"Four years now."

"And you hike around here pretty regular?" Back on point. She took a sip of the sweet tea and nodded approvingly.

"Nearly every day."

"You hike up around that little bridge on Byers' Creek sometimes?"

"Sometimes."

"Were you up there on Tuesday night? That night the big thunderstorm struck?"

"Yes."

Sheriff Render's eyebrows shot up. She set her glass down on a coaster. "You were?"

"Yes," he replied, compelled to be truthful for now.

"Did you see anything, hear anything unusual that night?"

She sat forward on the edge of her chair, fully attentive to Whit's remarks. Barney trundled from the woman to Whit and flopped down at his feet. Whit's left hand dropped and massaged the dog's thick neck.

"I heard a panther scream. Not a normal hike."

Sheriff Render was slowly nodding. "Do you know anything about Tory Cook's murder?"

"TV."

Silence. Then, the sheriff probing: "Do you *know* Tory Cook? Any problems with him?"

"Never met the man."

She rocked back and forth a little on the sofa, ignoring his evasion, bulldozing. "Did you see anyone else where you were hiking?"

"Hard rain. I stopped short of my hike. Panther screams."

"You didn't answer my question."

"I turned around and came back here."

"You have a moral obligation to report a crime," she said, an edge to her voice.

Whit said nothing, returning her gaze. Her lower jaw came a little bit forward as if she were growing restive. "It would be wrong not to help me out on this. If you saw anyone up there where you were hiking, you need to tell me."

"Do you have any suspects?" he asked.

"You should know that I can't comment on an ongoing investigation," she said, sitting up a little straighter, as if preparing to stand. She took another sip from the sweating glass of sweet tea and looked around the room.

"Probably a few troublemakers you can interview," he said. "The usual suspects."

A small smile played across Sheriff Render's face. "On another topic, I heard you had a run-in with J. D. Merrone."

"Hacker Merrone had a run-in with Barney."

"I would have liked to have seen that."

She looked at Whit. He looked back. Neither looked away.

"So, you're saying you didn't see anything the night of the storm, when you were hiking near the scene of the murder?"

"I sure *heard* something. Have you ever heard a panther scream?"

"Can't say I have. Well," she said, standing and tugging down on her pants legs, which had snugged up on her thighs, "if you remember anything, or discover anything that might help me with my investigation, don't hesitate." She set her glass back on the cork coaster on the coffee table.

"Thanks for stopping by."

"Thanks for the sweet tea. Nice to meet you," she said, extending her hand. "And nice to meet Barney, too." Della Render's hand was small but well muscled, firm of grip.

"Nice to meet *you*, Sheriff Render."

"I'll be seeing you," she said, crossing the room, opening the door, and stepping out to the porch. Whit followed her, shutting the door behind him to keep Barney inside.

"You're always welcome, Sheriff."

She dug a business card out of her shirt pocket and handed it to him. "If you change your mind and decide to do the right thing, give me a call."

He took the card and looked at it and stuffed it in his pocket. "Have a nice day."

Sheriff Render waved over her shoulder as she walked away, slipping on her sunglasses. Whit admired her backside, then thought it would be better to not follow up. *Surface appeal breeds disappointment.* She climbed into her cruiser, turned it around, and drove away, gravel crunching under tires until she reached the dirt road, then silence on the dusty surface.

When she finally turned on Panther Scream Road to head back to her office, Sheriff Render analyzed her introduction to Whit Coombs. She had indeed heard of him, an eccentric recluse hiding from people, but he did not strike her that way.

There was something about him: a fragility inside his confident exterior, his mildly attractive demeanor and appearance. He looked fit and strong, and smart, but maybe that was just the scholarly, rimless glasses. No, it was more than that. Something wise and knowing and, yes, experienced in those eyes.

He had evaded, parried, and dodged her questions, nonchalantly petting that gigantic dog. *And what a dog,* she thought. A beauty. And that made Whit Coombs even more appealing to her in some abstract way. A man who liked dogs.

But what was most appealing, she realized, was that the man knew something about the murder of Tory Cook. And she resolved to push and probe and badger the man until he provided full disclosure. She hit the accelerator and the cruiser lurched forward, the sheriff enjoying the surge of power and speed with no chance of a ticket.

Whit waited until silence returned, the cruiser long gone, then moseyed back into his cabin and, suddenly tired, decided to take a nap. He stretched out on his bed with his hands locked behind his head but could not sleep. He wondered why Sheriff Render had brought up the name of Hacker Merrone out of the blue, sandwiched inside questions of the murder up the trail.

She knows, he realized.

After a while, Barney jumped on the bed, curled up at the foot, and instantly fell asleep. Soon the big dog's deep, rhythmic snoring overcame the anxiety in Whit's mind, and he also napped, and for quite a while, too.

CHAPTER 8

"Nothing is more wretched than the
mind of a man conscious of guilt."
—Plautus

FOR THE NEXT TWO DAYS, Whit enjoyed the comfort of routine. He cleaned up the debris from the storm, tossing it into a brush pile that he would burn one day in autumn. He chopped more firewood, weeded his two flower gardens, mowed and trimmed his yard, tended to his vegetable garden, stayed inside during the heat of the day, and listened to music or read a good book. There was solace in repetition—a consistency to life that Whit clung to.

He hiked every day, taking Barney with him on those cooler early-evening forays into the mountainous woods. The big dog was mostly under voice control, even when he spied a squirrel. He would stay put, staring longingly after the squirrel, trembling in eagerness for the chase, and then Whit would release him, and Barney would take off like a brindle thunderbolt, confident that he would finally catch one of the elusive tree rats. Whit knew there was no harm in letting his dog enjoy being a dog—

treeing squirrels, sniffing in the underbrush with his tail wagging, and simply enjoying the hike.

Whit kept his eyes open for the black panther, or any other big cat that might be the one whose scream nearly separated Whit from his mind.

One late afternoon, downstream from the bridge at Byers' Creek, Whit came across the paw print of what he was pretty sure was a cougar: the classic asymmetrical, elongated print with four toe pads in a semicircle unique to mountain lions. No claw marks, of course, since they could retract those claws until needed. But this pad was bigger than he expected. He put his hand over the print to assess relative size.

Barney sniffed the prints and peered into the woods, his tail low and still, his nostrils twitching. The dog's behavior gave Whit chills, and he found himself pulling his handgun. But then Barney seemed to lose interest, so Whit holstered his weapon. He wondered what would happen if a cougar and Barney ever met. He suspected the cat would climb a tree, but it wasn't worth risking injury to the dog to find out. And so they turned slowly and retreated down the faint green trail, Whit constantly checking behind him.

When they returned to the cabin, Whit praised Barney for being so obedient, and the big dog slowly wagged his tail in response.

Whit knew that mountain lions, cougars, panthers, pumas, or whatever one chose to call them were beasts that lived solitary lives, and with no natural enemies except an occasional bear or a pack of wolves. Deep down, Whit was pleased they were nearby. The big cats were beautiful, sleek and sinewy, intelligent, and with strength under control. He admired them.

The next day, Sheriff Render came back. Whit saw her approach from his vantage point on the roof of his cabin where he was replacing a few cedar shakes near his satellite dish. It was late afternoon, and the temperatures had slid down into the low eighties. Still, he was dirty and sweaty, shirtless in his cutoffs and hiking shoes. He clanged down his aluminum extension ladder and ambled toward her patrol car as she got out.

She looked the same, except her uniform showed the results of a day's work, mostly outside in the heat, he guessed. Sweat darkened the front of her blouse at the throat, and she was two buttons down today. Her sunglasses hung from the pocket opposite her name tag. And she was still wearing the uniform shorts, Whit noticed. She noticed that he noticed and shrugged it off.

"Welcome back," he said. "Sorry for my appearance. Roof work."

"No problem," she said, giving him an appraising look.

"What can I do for you?"

"Just thought I'd update you on the murder investigation, and see if you had anything to add." She tucked a loose curl of blonde hair behind her ear.

"How's it going?"

With a sardonic smile she said, "I'm getting nowhere fast. I talked to Mr. Merrone and Mr. Butz and they don't know a thing about the murder, although they did admit to knowing Mr. Cook. They expressed sorrow over his murder, but their heartache struck me as insincere. Both have alibis for the night in question. No one in the mountains knows anything about it, but I'm inclined to think some of them do. Some*one* surely does."

"I can't help you." Whit rubbed his hands together, picked at a snagged fingernail.

She said, "That's just another way of not saying it."

The sheriff looked around—at the cabin, the clearing, the mountains. Shifted her weight. Said nothing for a while. Whit ran his fingers through his longish black hair, and Sheriff Render noticed the jagged scar on the right side of his head. Whit fingered his hair again, a nervous habit, the scar disappearing, and stuffed his hands in his pockets. He lifted his shoulders, dropped them. Sighed, determined not to break the silence with an offer to go inside and have some sweet tea.

"Are they bad men?" he finally asked.

"Been arrested a few times. Convicted on little stuff—public drunkenness, public urination, assault, petty theft. Minor drug stuff. Some bigger things. Assault charges that went away for lack of evidence or dropped charges from frightened victims," she said. "You know, the usual small-town incorrigibles. Funny, though. They did admit they had a beef with you about your dog. Mr. Merrone said Barney was *his* dog.

Also said he was considering filing a complaint about Barney, that he was dangerous and should be put down."

"So, what's the status of all that? He sounds confused about what he wants."

"There is nothing to support his claims. I told him to drop it."

Whit nodded.

The sheriff advanced to within two feet of Whit and said, "We sure have a good time talking around things, don't we?" Then she looked away and took in his flower gardens at the side of the cabin. He followed her gaze.

"You like flowers?" he asked.

"Partial to black-eyed Susans."

"You can take some with you," he said, turning and striding away, pulling out his pocket knife.

"No need, Mr. Coombs," she said to his bare back. She took a couple of steps after him and stopped.

Whit approached the flower garden and culled a dozen or so black-eyed Susans from the abundance. He bunched them together in one hand and returned to the sheriff, wiping the blade on his cutoffs and refolding his knife against his leg to stuff back into his pocket.

"Here," he said.

Sheriff Della Render smiled and said, "Thank you, Mr. Coombs. They're very nice."

"Welcome," he said, palming sweat away from his forehead and swiping his hand on his hip.

"You have my card?"

"I do."

"Well then, I'll be on my way. Don't hesitate to call me if you, if you. . ."

"I might," he said.

She nodded, turned, and headed back to her patrol car. Whit watched.

After she drove away, the car cruiser disappearing into the trees, he climbed back on the roof and finished the job, surprised that he still liked giving a woman some flowers.

CHAPTER 9

"Loneliness and the feeling of being
unwanted is the most terrible poverty."
—Mother Teresa

WHEN SHE FINISHED HER SHIFT and completed the notes from
her conversation with Whit, Sheriff Render left the department, drove to
the edge of Woodrow, and parked her cruiser on the white gravel drive
next to her bungalow.

She sat there for a while in the light of a fading late afternoon, glad
that her night-patrol shift didn't start for another week. She enjoyed being
home like a civilian at the end of the day, and some days the appeal of
regular hours and tedious work called to her, but not today. There was too
much going on in her head—an unlikely scenario if she were working at
the county clerk's office for eight hours, five days a week. Honest labor,
but work that over the years and decades tended to sand off the edges of
one's sense of adventure. She took a deep breath and slid out of her cruiser,
bouquet of black-eyed Susans in hand, and strode inside after retrieving
a few pieces of mail from her mailbox.

A yellow tabby rubbed against her legs. "I love you, too, Rex." He rubbed some more and then padded over to the front door, looked at her, and meowed. She let him out, saying, "Watch out for coyotes, big boy." He scooted. She closed the door and sauntered into her kitchen.

After placing her flowers in a vase, Render set hot water going for tea, then entered her bedroom and placed her holstered Glock 9 on the dresser, next to her daughter's high school graduation photo. She removed her badge from the regulation blouse and set it next to the handgun. Then she did the same with her name tag. She undressed and tossed her uniform into a dirty clothes basket. She slipped on a pair of blue pajama bottoms, stepped in front of her full-length mirror, and removed her bra. "Not bad, girl," she said, then wondered if Whit Coombs looked with as much interest at her chest as she had at his that afternoon.

A sheen of sweat had highlighted the sleek muscles of Whit Coombs' tan, lean chest, and the vague hint of a possible six-pack didn't detract one bit from her impression of him. *Impressive for a man his age, and what is his age in the first place? Fifties?*

She slipped on a baggy, purple Western Carolina University Alumni T-shirt with the head of an irritable feline under the letters *WCU*. Her teapot was whistling now, and she poured the hot water into a big mug with a cinnamon-apple tea bag. Reaching into an overhead cabinet, she withdrew a bottle of Maker's Mark, and added a dollop of the whiskey to her tea, for seasoning.

In her living room, she plopped into a recliner and sorted through her mail. Nothing important but the monthly report of her daughter, confined for five years now in a private hospital in Asheville. The girl existed in a constant vegetative state from head trauma suffered from an automobile accident involving a drunk driver and a wet, curvy mountain road on a crisp October night.

Sheriff Render was first at the scene because she had been the one in hot pursuit of the speeding, erratic pickup truck that skidded into the oncoming lane and into her daughter's Celica. The collision sounded like a bomb going off. The drunk driver was dead. Her daughter might as well be, Render often thought. When she went through the persistent "what-ifs" in her mind, it was peculiar how she always saw in vivid detail the fiery autumn leaves stuck to the wet, black surface of the road at the accident scene. But she could not remember the crushed vehicles—a mercy.

Her husband, unable to deal with Hayley's condition, coupled with embedded resentment of Della's love for her work, now lived in California with his new wife and their child. The damaged daughter and Della's decision to continue in law enforcement gave him excuses to leave before Christmas that year, the divorce papers appearing soon after.

Her daughter's condition remained "stable," another word for "unchanged." Della's own personal observations from multiple visits confirmed the status report. She refolded the letter and set it aside and picked up her cup of tea and sipped. It was good. Cradling the cup in one hand, with the other she pulled the lever that raised the chair's footrest. Now holding the cup in two hands, she drank again and thought about her conversation with Whit Coombs.

Despite his physical appeal, Coombs made Render angry. They both knew that he knew something about the murder of Tory Cook, but he still wasn't coming forward.

He didn't look like a man who could be intimidated by Merrone and Butz, even though they could be intimidating. There was something in Coombs's background that spoke of resilience, character, even a bit of danger. So why was he hesitant in helping her?

Render took another sip of her fortified tea. Was Coombs so committed to his privacy that he would overlook a murder he had witnessed with his own eyes? Would he be that self-concerned?

She finished her tea, rose, and walked into her kitchen, junk mail in one hand. She dumped the mail in the trash can under the sink, then glanced at the clock on the microwave and understood why her stomach was growling. She had skipped lunch, and now her body was reminding her it needed fuel.

In short order she heated up leftover tuna casserole and a thick slice of homemade bread. She slathered butter on the bread and watched it melt, opened a bottle of Heineken, and poured the beer into a frosted mug from the freezer. Then she took her meal back to the living room and the recliner.

Later, after showering and changing into fresh pajamas, she watched two episodes of a Brit detective series on Acorn while enjoying another Heineken. Suddenly tired, Della turned off lights around the house, then opened her back door and called out, "Come home, Rex babe. Come on, boy." The cat appeared and came in purring, a welcome companion and agreeable conversationalist. Della climbed into bed. But she could not sleep. There was something about Whit Coombs that she could not figure, and she was good at reading people. At times her life had depended on it.

Two hours of sleeplessness followed. And then it came to her, and she knew what it was she had not been able to identify. Whit Coombs was broken inside. She knew what that felt like. When she realized his pain, she shook her head, punched her pillow into proper shape, and fell asleep, the cat pressed warm and purring against the small of her back.

CHAPTER 10

"Denial, panic, threats, anger—those are
very human responses to feeling guilt."
—Joshua Oppenheimer

WHIT KISSED THE INSIDE of her wrists, her throat, said he was sorry. She pushed him back, her fingers tipped with bloody thorns, glared at him with anger and disappointment, turned her skeletal body away, said "Coward" and "Failure" and "Liar" over her bony shoulder, and faded out.

Barney was licking Whit's sweaty face, nudging him back to wakefulness in the pitch dark of his bedroom in the cabin in the mountains.

"Good dog, good boy," he mumbled, sitting up.

The big dog stared at Whit for a moment, wagged his tail, and retreated to the foot of the bed and threw himself down. Soon he was snoring. *He* is *a good dog*, Whit thought. If only he had intervened a bit sooner.

There were no pictures of her, of *them*, in the cabin. Whit saw no reason to kick-start the pain with photos of Susan, of them together. As the years passed, he struggled to remember what she looked like, what she felt like, the nuances of her love for life, and that brought on more guilt. Sometimes he would go days without thinking about her, but she was always there, alive in the nightmare, waiting to dig away at the white scar of healing and reopen it to the oozing of his emotional blood. And he knew he deserved it.

He pondered his past, reliving the night he had gone back on his word, refusing to smother his Susan to death. She had made him promise that if she had three consecutive days of praying she would die, he would take the pillow and put it over her face.

She waited a fourth, then a fifth day. She told him it was time.

The woman Whit loved and had been married to for seventeen years had suffered for two years, the agony of bone cancer having metastasized into her organs. And so, after two bottles of wine one night, they made their mutual pledge about the pillow. No razor, handgun, poison, or leaping from a precipice. No drugs. She insisted on being awake at the very end of her life.

"If I tried any of those methods, I'd probably screw up and be a failed suicide, a quadriplegic who spits bitterness at people who love me. No thanks. The pillow would work. You could make sure, Whit. Then you could hide the body," she said, "and when people ask, 'Where's Susan?' you could just say, 'She left me.'"

"No one would doubt that," Whit said. "They'd just wonder why you didn't leave me sooner."

She grinned and gooched him in the ribs when he said that.

When the time came, they prayed together, asking forgiveness prior to the act, kissed. She reclined in her favorite jammies, the ones with Professor McGonagall's face on them, winked at Whit and said, "Proceed, my love."

He did not.

She told him he must, if he loved her and honored their promises. That she would not resist except for a brief, involuntary flutter of activity, her body's response to its innate desire to live, but then her force of mind would let her give up.

He refused.

She pled again, calling on their love and commitment to each other, their deep promises she called "holy."

"I can't do it," he said to his wife.

"I am furious with you!"

"I won't kill you," he said. "I won't take your life."

For the next few days in the hospice, he refused to leave when she told him—when none of the staff could hear—to get the hell out. That he was condemning her to more agony. The disease had made her once athletic body a memory. She would not take pain medication. She said she wanted to embrace life to the very end, even thought the tidal waves of teeth-chattering pain wracked her as she pressed her hands to her face to muffle her guttural screams.

At the very end, after he had taken her back home to die, respecting that last wish of hers, she glared at Whit and said, "Coward" and "Failure." Then she took in a half breath and was gone, her hands slowly falling away from her face, like pages in an open book.

The nightmare never went away. He hoped and prayed that the years would erode his dread of remembering, or even cancel out any tendrils of guilt thriving in his mind, but they did not. The torment was never resolved.

There were no children.

He never stopped loving her. He never stopped feeling guilty.

And so, when he met other women, attractive, smart and funny, he would not allow himself to go beyond that first step of reserved politeness. He realized he was attracted to Della Render, but that interest would have to be buried. Too much to go wrong, too little to go right. And the fact that she could get him in trouble made a second step, beyond a cold glass of sweet tea or a rough bouquet of black-eyed Susans, impossible.

This night, he was not able to go back to sleep, even with the soothing rumble of Barney's snoring in the dark.

When soft light suffused the cabin with a faint, pink sunrise, Whit rolled out of bed, fell to his knees, and prayed, "Lord Jesus, forgive me, a miserable sinner." And then he set to his breakfast for himself, and duties to his dog.

Over the years, Whit had learned that taking on some project immediately after the nightmare, a project requiring serious concentration, helped him focus his mind on something other than Susan's haunting indictment. One year, he hunted rattlesnakes, completely forgetting about Susan for an afternoon. At the end of the day, he had six fat, dead diamondbacks in his gunny sack. He skinned and cleaned them and fried them in his deep fat fryer. And ate them, thereafter deciding that rattlesnake meat was an acquired taste that he did not want to acquire.

Another time, just a year or so before he bought the cabin, he awoke from the nightmare and drove into Asheville and entered a local tough-man contest. He won his first two bouts but lost decisively in the third contest to a man who weighed exactly twice as much as Whit. And who threw him out of the ring after Whit had bloodied the man's nose. Landing on the backs of a row of permanent wooden seats generated two broken ribs. Whit liked the pain that came with each breath. This helped him to forget, too, for a while.

Now, because of his aversion to strangers, and crowds of strangers, he decided to drive up to Junaluska Falls and mingle with the thousands of people attending the annual Bluegrass Music Festival that took place every June in the small mountain village. With just under 1,000 inhabitants in the village itself, the event typically drew ten times that many for the festival.

Whit gave Barney an airing, fixed himself a light breakfast of cheese grits, sausage patties, and a buttermilk biscuit with honey, along with his coffee, and then hit the road with his friend, knowing Barney would attract plenty of attention. That, of course, forced Whit to be sociable with all his strength. And forget about Susan, at least for a while.

And so, this day, Barney and Whit crept the three miles out to Screaming Panther Road, where Whit took a right and soon after left the crumbling road for a narrow, smooth blacktop, cruising along at a steady fifty-five miles per hour, enjoying the verdant, abundant tunnel of old trees canopied over the highway and bushes and wildflowers thick along the side of the road.

Just outside of Junaluska Falls, Whit saw campsites with tents, motor homes, and travel trailers scattered along the roadside. He recoiled from the evidence of crowds and considered turning around. If there had been a convenient wide spot along the blacktop, he would have. But there was no room. So he continued on into town, banners everywhere touting a 1K fun run, a 5K road race, a street dance, and bluegrass music concerts at the downtown pavilion.

After cruising slowly around the village, he found a front yard offering all-day parking for just twenty dollars. He took the last space, gave the bearded old man on his front porch the money, then retrieved Barney from the passenger seat and strolled toward the sound of banjos coming from down the narrow street. Since the big dog was obedient, he was unleashed as he strode alongside Whit, easing into the crowd.

Some people, mostly men, frowned and edged away when they saw Barney. Women tended to smile and want to pet him, which Whit allowed with a nod to their hesitant entreaties. It was easy to talk about his dog: his age, breed, disposition, weight. Barney loved it and found himself with several admirers, who ran to get friends to come see the giant, gentle dog with the wagging tail. Whit strolled in the bright sunshine of the morning, taking in the displays and listening to the bluegrass.

He moseyed along untempted by the funnel cakes or festival T-shirts or hand-carved wooden whistles. He passed an artist's renderings of different subjects on black felt—a naked woman, a snarling leopard, and Elvis—and kept walking.

He did stop to look at several simply framed oil paintings of mountain landscapes displayed on three-legged racks in front of a small, yellow tent. The vibrant colors, light, and composition stopped him at first glance. At second glance, he liked them even more. No one else was looking.

"So, what do you think?"

Whit turned and took in a woman with flaming-red hair streaked with gray, an emerald-green T-shirt, and faded blue jeans. Her eyes matched her T-shirt. The woman's face was tan, and her hair was pulled back into a single braid that dropped halfway down her back. Her arms were folded under an abundant bosom. She seemed to be about Whit's age.

"I like them all," he said. Barney sat and gazed around at the people passing by, his tail wagging briefly every time a passerby noticed him.

"But *why* do you like them?"

He returned his gaze to the oils. "There is light, strong colors. I don't know much about art, but. . . "

"But you know what you like?"

"Yes."

She said, "If an outlaw put a gun to your head and ordered you to take one home, which would it be?"

Whit glanced back at the woman, then said, "That one," pointing to a rendering of the Blue Ridge Mountains in autumn.

"Hmmm."

"So," he said, "how long have you been painting?"

The woman laughed. "That obvious, huh?"

He said, "At first I wasn't sure. Then I was."

"My name is Beverly Andreeson, but my friends call me Bev, and I've been painting all my life, at least since, well, I guess you could say I've been painting quite a while."

"I'm Whit Coombs," he said.

She took his hand. They shook with strength into strength and let go. "And I assume this magnificent animal is yours?"

"His name is Barney."

"Love that name. It fits, big and affable. Look at those eyes."

Whit nodded, smiled, and gazed down at Barney. Easier than talking with a woman.

They turned their attention back to the paintings. Whit didn't know what else to say, so he remained silent. It was quiet, except for the crowd meandering about. Then Barney growled. Whit turned to his dog.

A fat, sunburned boy was poking the stick from a consumed corn dog at Barney's face. The couple with him, both as stuffed as a tick on a hog, were laughing. The boy started to poke at Barney again, the big dog pulling back.

"Stop that!" Whit said.

"He's just playin', for chrissakes," the man said. The boy moved his pointed stick toward Barney again.

"Back off," Whit said, stepping toward the boy, who jumped behind his mother and started crying. The woman, like her son and husband, was sunburned, her flimsy tank top exposing red skin. Tattoos played along her collarbones, one being an arrow pointing down and proclaiming, *This way to fun!*

The man, who was also dressed in a baggy tank top, along with an Atlanta Braves cap, flip-flops, and cargo pants that exposed milk-white calves, said, "You leave my boy alone, pal." He took a step toward Whit.

"He needs to leave my dog alone. You're lucky he's good natured."

"We'll see," the man said. And then he shoved Barney hard with his foot.

In an instant, Barney sprang with his paws against the man's chest, staggering him back several steps before he tripped over his corpulent son. Both fell backwards and landed hard on the pavement. Barney, now wagging his tail, brought his muzzle within inches of the fallen man's face.

"Barney! No!" Whit said, and the dog immediately bounded back to Whit's side and sat down, looking up imploringly at Whit, who praised him, petting his head and saying, "Good dog, good dog."

"'Good dog' like hell!" the man yelled, scrambling to his feet in front of the growing crowd viewing the spectacle.

"Don't take no shit offa him, Ray!" screamed the wife.

Whit pointed a finger at the man and said, his voice calm, "You get away from us."

Ray muttered, "Shit" and then said, "I won't forget this, boy."

The little family shuffled away, the man glaring over his shoulder while his woman flashed a middle finger over her shoulder, an artistic gesture replicated by the little boy.

"That was interesting," Bev said as Whit stroked Barney.

"I'd like to buy that one," Whit said, pointing at the painting they had been enjoying.

"Well, thank you!" she said. She moved to the rack and removed the work.

Whit pulled out his wallet and sorted out a variety of bills that came to 400 dollars. He gave her the money. "That's what the sign says, isn't it?"

"I could give you a discount for cash," she said, handing over the painting.

"No need. I've got to go now."

"But first, may I trouble you for your address so I can send you my newsletter? It's about upcoming shows, what I'm working on, art gossip." She handed Whit a notebook open to a written list of names and addresses. "And your email and phone number, too, please."

Whit wrote his address on the first blank line and handed the notebook back.

Bev peered at the notebook and said, "You forgot your email and phone number."

"I don't have those."

He took the painting, thanked her, and left with his dog, leaving the artist with a stunned look on her face and cash in her hand.

"I'll be damned," she said.

CHAPTER 11

"It's true that no child is born knowing there's an
evil thing. You learn what is ugly."

—Lucy Dacus

THE FIRST TIME she was raped, she was five years old. Her favorite
uncle, charming Uncle Melvin, stayed behind with her during the family
reunion at the lake. Everyone else was down at the dock, children jumping
in the water and splashing the grown-ups. The two of them stayed behind
because she liked stories and he promised to read to her from her favorite
book, *For Horse-Crazy Girls Only*. He did for a little while; then he closed
the book.

He reached out for her, telling her it was okay, a game for sweet girls.
She told him it hurt, but he said sometimes little girls had to hurt because
it made them prettier. "You can't be a princess without a little pain," he told
her. Uncle Melvin said it would be their secret and she said, "Okay, Uncle
Melvin" through her sniffles. He said if she didn't tell anyone, he'd get her a
horse for her twelfth birthday. And he said if she did tell, he would take his
knife to her face. She believed and remained stone silent about their secret.

The next times were in her bedroom with her favorite model horses looking on, her bedroom with the flowery wallpaper and horse posters and the frilly curtains and all the other books about girls and horses. At first it was Uncle Melvin, then one of her cousins, then a boy from the neighborhood who was cute and told her she was pretty, proving what Uncle Melvin said. Uncle Melvin was a regular.

Beverly never broke her silence about their secret, even though twelve came and went and no horse appeared.

The games stopped when she began cutting herself. Her parents never knew why she was that crazy, or at least that's what they told themselves. Not their fault, for sure. Beverly was just a disturbed adolescent girl with screwy female emotions they weren't willing to accommodate in their own lives. "Hormones," they said, to comfort themselves. When they dropped her off at the Willows everyone cried, except Beverly.

After she was introduced to art therapy, she dropped everything else that interested her and focused on painting. The ditsy, braless art teacher with the Janis Joplin T-shirt and pungent body odor who came by the facility once a week told Beverly she had "great aptitude."

The young artist was eighteen when she signed herself out of the Willows. She secured a job in an artist-supplies business in a small town miles and miles away, and rented a room over the store. She never saw her parents again, which was okay by them. So embarrassing to have a daughter like that anyway. They made no attempt to find her. They were sure she'd be okay. They smiled and said, "God's will" and spent extra time with their boys.

Her artistic strengths shifted over time from bleak winter landscapes to rich colors of the other seasons. Her weakness was portraits, especially of men—she could never get their faces right, always a bit askew. She took classes at the community college and sold two paintings when she was in her mid-twenties. She went on to a four-year college as an art major on scholarship, and her development soared. She sold a few more paintings.

And then it happened again. A custodian in the art department in his sour-smelling closet, her back pressed against a damp mop. He called her a name and kicked her out of the building and promised he'd kill her if she told anyone, so she didn't. Who'd believe her? And what would it matter?

So she ran away, and ran away again. Years later, she found herself in an artists' colony near Black Mountain, North Carolina. She took that pleasant experience as a springboard to a career as a landscape artist, moving into her upstairs apartment in Woodrow, where she was assaulted one night years ago by J. D. Merrone and Buford Butz after they followed her home from a pub where she had gone with a girlfriend to relax and enjoy a glass of white wine and a local band.

She told no one, just as before. Shame. Guilt. (What did she do, or say, and wear?) Still, she endured, fought despair, drank, and kept painting. Over the years in North Carolina, she regained herself, stabilized, and began to carve out a good life. She even thought about some men without chilling apprehension; nice men—her agent, the maintenance man at the Honda dealership, her grumpy but sweet landlord.

She did not run away again.

And now there was Whit Coombs, shy, a bit damaged like her, she thought, who appreciated her work but did not know why. In any case, she was grateful for the sale and pleased for the chance meeting with her newest patron.

She surprised herself when she realized she wouldn't object to seeing him again. Someday.

CHAPTER 12

"Beware the barrenness of an empty life."
—Confucious

"IT'S A GIFT TO BE SIMPLE," goes the old Shaker hymn, and Whit believed it and lived it. Things he did not possess helped make Whit Coombs's life full. No cell phone, social media, or accountability to others. No debt. No mail to speak of. Addition by subtraction.

He kept up with his vegetable garden, two blueberry bushes, and a pair of fig trees, enjoying the benefits of good food raised by his own hand. Planting, watering, protecting—even weeding was a pleasure. And now, late in the summer, evenings found him lounging in one of his Adirondack chairs on the back deck after dinner, his feet up on a little wooden footstool, relaxing with a glass of wine in his hand and his friend at his feet.

The TV and radio news programs had gradually quit mentioning the murder of Tory Cook, just as Whit expected. No one was going to rat out Merrone or Butz. Those who might know something were either afraid of retribution, or else they just didn't care about one more feud in the high country settled by a knife or gun or club. With no leads, there was little for the law to do but hope that someday, something useful would emerge from their investigation.

That investigation is probably nothing more than a cold case now, Whit thought. He sipped some more wine and retrieved a half dozen almonds from a can, popping them into his mouth two or three at a time, then giving Barney a couple.

Whit gazed across the smooth blue lake to the trees on the far side, only their tops in the sunshine now, the Blue Ridge providing a backdrop in the distance. The sun slipped slowly behind the mountains behind Whit to the west, and he found himself taking comfort in the simple beauty of place. He was content but for the one little snag still staving off complete serenity: what he had seen on the primitive bridge across Byers' Creek that night several weeks ago now.

Even as the night slipped into the shadows of memory, he couldn't quite shake it—that sense that maybe he should say something to Sheriff Render. But that thought always swung back around to the logic of his reasons. His word against theirs, a slick lawyer undermining what Whit knew he had seen, and then the fact that the two men would never let it go if he testified against them.

Better to just release it and hope something bad happened to Hacker and Buford. *Let God deal with those two.* He would anyway, sooner or later. In the meantime, Whit enjoyed his solitude, a gift that sometimes felt like loneliness. An acceptable tradeoff.

His mind drifted again to Sheriff Della Render. He had not seen her in weeks, and he wondered what she was up to. Even though she didn't look it, her demeanor made him think of a pitbull. She knew he had seen something, and he knew she would never give up. He poured himself another glass of wine, shook out the last of the almonds into his hand, and shared them with Barney.

The big dog heard the approaching pickup truck seconds before Whit.

"Shit," Whit muttered, annoyed at the interruption. Easing to his feet, he followed Barney around the side of the cabin to the front yard.

He recognized the truck coming to a stop in the gravel area, and the two men who got out. "Speak of the devil and he appears," Whit muttered.

Whit stood halfway between his front porch and the parked truck, Barney at his side, a low, barely audible growl rumbling deep in his thick chest.

"What can I do for you boys?" Whit asked.

"Well," Hacker said, the high-pitched voice amusing Whit, "you could invite us into your nice little cabin and offer us a beer. How's that?"

Whit smiled and shook his head.

The two men ambled up to Whit and stopped about ten feet short when Barney's growl increased. Whit put his hand on Barney's head, and the dog went silent, his brown eyes locked onto the pair of visitors.

"We heard you like to hike in the mountains. That right?" Hacker asked, hooking his thumbs in the front pockets of his jeans.

Whit said nothing.

Butz snickered and said, "And we heard you like to hike up in there *at night* sometimes. Right?"

When Whit remained silent, Hacker raised his voice a little and said, "I guess you heard about poor Tory Cook being killed up north on the Byers' Creek bridge. And we was wonderin' if maybe you might have been hiking up there that night when somethin' turrible happened to that boy."

Barney, still sitting at Whit's side, began to tremble at the slight uptick in Hacker's voice.

"Anything else I can help you boys with?" Whit asked. He removed his rimless glasses and cleaned them with the hem of his shirt.

Hacker chuckled, an unkind, sinister chuckle. "I guess not, if you gonna be so fuckin' stone mouthed about it. We're guessin' maybe you was up there that night. We jus' want you to understand you better keep your piehole shut like a good boy, or somethin' unpleasant could happen to you and that mutt there. And I ain't afraid of you or that piece of shit at your side."

Whit said nothing, maintaining eye contact.

"Well, boy, I guess we understand each other," Butz said. "Just leave things be and you'll be just fine. Won't have to worry about your mutt getting shot, or your cabin burnin' down, or—"

Hacker backhanded Butz across his narrow chest. "Shut the fuck up, Buford!"

The smaller man stumbled back a couple of steps, his mouth falling open and his face twisted. He looked imploringly at Hacker, who ignored him.

Barney growled, and Whit settled his hand on the dog's broad skull once more. Barney went silent, but he was trembling again.

"Shove off," Whit said.

The two men looked surprised. Then Hacker said, "We gone, but you never know when we'll come visitin' again. You lack a little in the hospitality department, boy. Come on, Buford."

With that, the two men turned and slouched back to the pickup truck, the one Hacker was driving the night they murdered Tory Cook. They flipped on their headlights as they pulled away in the growing darkness.

Whit watched the one red taillight disappear around the corner of the dirt trail leading to Panther Scream Road. He listened until the sound of the truck faded completely, then walked back around the cabin to the deck, Barney at his side, wagging his big tail.

Whit groaned as he settled back in his wooden chair. Barney flopped down at his master's feet. More wine and peaceful contemplation followed as the trees across the lake faded in the darkness, ghostlike, and the clear, black skies tossed down starlight reflected on the blue lake like tiny bits of burning magnesium.

Whit knew men like Merrone and Butz. They would nick and nibble and try to intimidate, and if that didn't work, they'd get physical.

He drank the last of the wine and sighed and sat with his friend for a spell in the privacy of the night, and then they ambled inside together, and to bed. Barney fell asleep quickly, his soft snoring soothing at Whit's feet.

Whit did not sleep, praying he would not have to do what he knew how to do.

CHAPTER 13

"The greatest threat is not to kill but to let live."
—James Oliver Curdwood, *The Grizzly King*

AUTUMN GRADUALLY SLIPPED into the highlands like a beautiful, colorful, mature woman, confident that even her wrinkles were sexy. Summer, a sunny, sassy girl without limitations, looked over her shoulder at the color glowing on the tips of trees at the higher elevations, took the hint, and strolled away, nonchalantly tapping her floppy straw hat against her leg. Chilly nights took over from still-hot days.

The shifting weather suited Whit Coombs.

His hikes were good year-round but at their best in the fall when the trees traded in their shades of green for a more colorful palate of yellow and orange, red and brown. The colors were so beautiful Whit ached as he took them in, knowing how transitory their brilliance would be. The colors mirrored the ones in the painting that artist sold him. He still had the business card she had pressed into his hand. It rested on the mantel where he could look at it.

Whit was finishing up the harvesting of his garden when September crept through the back door unannounced. Blueberries were tapering off, figs were nearly gone, and his other plants hunched their shoulders in anticipation of winter. The cold nights helped with the transition from one season to the next, and the first frost a few weeks later sealed the deal.

With less work to do in the vegetable and flower gardens, Whit now had more time to justify the big-screen TV he purchased a while back. He loved college football and scheduled his trips to town and recreational outings with Barney so as not to interfere with his football-watching schedule.

In the past, he had gone in person to see the games. One trip to Cullowhee to watch the Western Carolina Catamounts play, and another to Boone to take in an Appalachian State Mountaineers game. But in Boone, the home team's mascot, dressed like Daniel Boone himself, fired his loud musket after every ASU score, and there were several. So Whit had to leave at halftime, his jitters shaken loose by gunfire. Anyway, he liked watching the games by himself better than taking them in personally. Replays, close-ups, and scores from around the nation only added to the telecasts.

The new football season helped distract him from the threatening visit from Merrone and Butz. He knew they would come by again, if only to escalate the implied danger to him if he talked too much with local law enforcement. They didn't know Sheriff Render had stopped by twice, Whit revealing nothing to her about what he had seen. They also didn't know that he kept his revolver handy in case they ever showed up again. And then they did.

It was deep into September one late afternoon, following a relaxing day for Whit. After stacking firewood by the front door and placing a few logs in the cold fireplace for later, he had given himself the afternoon off, settling into a good book, his reading taking up most of the remaining daylight. Then he prepared dinner and was about to sit down to eat when he heard the familiar sound of Hacker's pickup truck.

Whit tucked his handgun into the back of his jeans and bloused over his flannel shirt, even as Barney slid from his place on the sofa and joined him outside at the front door. The truck's headlights shone brightly in the deepening shadows and spotlighted Whit and Barney. Hacker and Buford emerged from the truck's cab, leaving the engine running.

Whit walked out a bit from the cabin, Barney at his side. When Whit stopped, so did the big dog. He sat beside Whit, softly growling.

"How the hell are ya?" Hacker asked, his tone jovial, confident. Whit was glad he had his gun handy. He had learned over the years such an attitude meant trouble. He said nothing.

"You and that fucking dog too good to answer back?" Butz sneered.

Hacker turned halfway back to the truck, then said, "I got somethin' that might loosen your tongues a little, one way or another." And he started for the bed of the truck.

"Got a *coupla* somethin's for y'all, to be sure," Buford cackled.

There was the sound of heavy chains falling onto the metal bed, and then two big dogs appeared around the front of the pickup, snarling and straining at the leashes Hacker had wrapped around his hand. He said, "I left the headlights on so we can be sure to see what's comin' next for you and that piece-of-shit mutt of yours, growling at me. Yeah, I can hear 'im. Well, here's somethin' for him to growl at!"

With that, Hacker released the dogs—big and sturdy, of no breed in particular, but about the size of Rottweilers—and they made for Barney. Whit reached behind him and drew his gun.

The big dogs set on Barney, snarling as Barney met their charge with yelps of pain and snarls of his own. Quickly, they had him down, Barney biting and kicking. Whit ran up to the fray and fired two shots into the left chest of the bigger of the two dogs.

He turned to shoot the other, but Barney had regained his feet, clamped down on the remaining dog's shoulder, and flipped it onto its back, blood spraying from multiple wounds on both animals. Barney latched onto its foreleg.

The sound of the bone breaking followed. Barney let go of the leg and muzzled down on the dog's throat, holding the remaining attacker down and pinning him like a wrestler, not closing his jaws for the kill. Both dogs were bloodied, but Barney had full command.

"Barney, NO!" Whit shouted, and the big dog released and came to his side. The other dog writhed in pain and finally dragged itself away, foreleg dangling. Barney sat down hard, panting, at Whit's side. "Good dog, good dog!" Barney's tail thumped a little.

"You sonuvabitch, Coombs! I'll kill you for this," Hacker shouted, his normal high-pitched voice higher now. "You killed my best dog, and this one's gonna hafta be put down now."

"Yeah!" Butz shouted.

As the crippled dog came to Hacker, he delivered a vicious kick to its ribs. The dog yelped and cringed, still hobbling on just three sound legs. Hacker turned to Butz and told him to dump the dog in the back of the truck. While Buford dragged the dog, Merrone strode toward where the dogs had fought.

"Take this one, too," Whit said. He held the .38 at his side.

Merrone squatted down and picked up the bloody, dead dog and heaved it over his shoulder, stood, staggered a little, pointed a finger at Whit. "You're a dead man, Coombs. And your dog's gonna join you."

"Get off my property and leave us alone," Whit said, his voice calm.

After the men had left, Whit took Barney inside and stood him under a good overhead light. He examined the big dog, using cotton swabs and hydrogen peroxide to clean multiple fang marks on the dog's throat, where his thick folds of heavy skin kept the bites from anything vital. Other punctures in the shoulders were tended to, as was a ragged ear. Barney thumped his tail the whole time.

When he finished, Whit gave Barney a hamburger and French fries from the plate on the kitchen counter, said, "Good dog, Barney," and let him loose. The big dog lumbered into the bedroom and jumped up on the bed. In a matter of minutes, he was asleep and snoring.

"Clean conscience, big fella," Whit said.

In the morning, the two of them drove to Woodrow to see their vet, Dr. Henry Moreland. Whit had his reloaded revolver in the glove compartment.

They did not have an appointment, so they had to wait their turn, enduring cautious glances from other clients who pulled their pets closer while the good doctor treated two cats, a dachshund, and a white mongrel bitch with three puppies. When it was his turn, Whit took Barney on a leash into the examining room where Dr. Moreland's vet tech led them.

"You did well cleaning him up," Moreland said after he tended to Barney, who remained calm throughout the process. "And I think those stitches in his ear will keep it looking close to normal again. He is such a good dog," he said, rubbing Barney between his shoulder blades. "Bring him in if he seems 'off.' You know, if he stops wagging his tail. You can take the stitches out in a few days. Now, mind telling me what happened?"

Whit told Dr. Moreland most of the truth. Then he paid his bill, headed outside with his dog, and opened the passenger door for Barney, who hopped happily onto the shotgun seat.

A woman's voice asked, "What happened to Barney?"

Whit turned to the speaker. "Mornin', Sheriff Render."

She strode over to the truck's window and put her hand inside. Barney licked her fingers and wagged his tail while she cooed softly to him. She turned back to Whit.

"Well?" she said, jerking her head toward the truck.

"Merrone and his buddy came by last night. Set two dogs on Barney. I think I was next. I shot one and Barney took care of the other. Merrone said he'd have to put it down."

"Do you want to make a report, file a complaint, press charges?"

"No."

She rolled her eyes. "What did they want?"

"Intimidation. Second visit."

A loaded lumber truck rolled by, gears crashing, its long load of tree trunks bouncing lightly off the back end, red flag and all. Whit smelled the tangy sap in the clear mountain air.

"What did they want the first time?" Sheriff Render watched the truck disappear, then turned back to Whit. He noticed her gray eyes, the keen intelligence, the femaleness of them.

"Pretty much what you wanted. Answers to questions about that night."

"I'm glad you're okay. Barney going to be okay, too?"

"Sure."

Render waved at a patrol car heading out on rounds. The deputy waved back. "It's rumored that Merrone runs a dogfighting ring up in the hollers," she said. "He takes dogs in and feeds them gunpowder and sets them on cats and smaller dogs to train them for fighting. Can't quite catch him at it, but I will."

"Gunpowder?"

"Supposed to make them meaner," she said.

"What's the penalty around here for dogfighting?"

"It's a Class H felony, good for four to twenty-five months in jail, depending," she said.

"Should be more than that. I hate good animals being ruined."

"That's one thing we agree on, Mr. Coombs," she replied.

"Anything on the Tory Cook case?" Whit asked, immediately wishing he'd just kept his mouth shut. She'd wonder why he was so interested.

"Nope. Still investigating," she said, an edge to her voice, a little extra flash in the gray eyes. "I don't suppose you might have anything to add that would move things along to a fair and just conclusion, do you?"

"No."

"You know something, Mr. Coombs? You are holding out information that just might be useful in convicting whoever it was that murdered that poor man. I just don't get it. Maybe you think you've attained some moral high ground where you decide what's right and wrong, what's good and true, and to hell with the rest of us groveling around in the mud of convention. Now, if you're holding back because those men are threatening, it's okay to be afraid. I could offer you some protection. I could have a deputy patrol more around your place, maybe park back in the trees now and then and watch out for you."

"No, thanks," he said, "but I appreciate it."

She sighed. "Keep in touch, Mr. Coombs."

Whit gave her a slight nod, climbed in his truck, and drove away with his dog beside him, amused that the sheriff just didn't get it; Hacker and Butz were the ones who should be fearful.

And what he took away from his conversation with Sheriff Render was how badly he wanted to kiss her mouth.

CHAPTER 14

"God loves you unconditionally, as you are not
as you should be, because nobody is as they should be."
—Brennan Manning

THE CHURCH WAS CINDER BLOCK, painted white with a simple cross atop the green metal roof. The late-afternoon sun was shining as a skinny man mowed the front yard. The building itself was set back off the narrow blacktop road. A gravel parking lot separated the church from a tidy cemetery, erect tombstones sitting up straight, as if paying attention to life. Out front, a neatly lettered white sign read *God's Grace Church* in black letters.

Whit pulled into the parking lot and stopped. He took in the smell of cut grass. Probably the last go-around of the season. A scattering of colorful leaves carpeted the lawn. The man mowing looked up, killed the power. He sauntered over to the F-150 as Whit got out.

"You've been here before," the man said, extending his hand. "Jimmy Fogel, pastor. You're Whit Coombs."

"It's been nearly a year," Whit said, shaking hands. "How do you . . . ?"

"Easy to remember names when the congregation's compact. See, there's something good in everything." The man laughed and let go. "What's the occasion?"

Whit looked around at the church, the cemetery, the ridge of wooded mountains snug up against the back of the property. The outhouse. He said, "I need to get something off my chest. If I do that, you can't tell anyone, can you?"

Jimmy Fogel smiled again and said, "Nossir, and you mean the clergy–penitent privilege. It must be a private conversation and not intended for further disclosure."

Whit cocked his head. "Again?"

"If you tell me something in confidence, I will never tell anyone else, including state and local law enforcement, the United States government, even the IRS."

Whit nodded. "Can I tell you now?"

"Of course," Fogel said. "Let's go inside. It's cooler."

They turned and strolled together to the front of the church. Pastor Fogel pulled the door open and gestured for Whit to go ahead. Inside, padded folding chairs and an altar stood in front of a large, wooden cross on the wall. Tall windows on the sides, a big window behind the altar. Abundant light. Cool and silent. Clean.

Whit took a seat and looked at his hands in his lap. Pastor Fogel sat in the same row with one chair separating them. He threw his arm over the back of the middle chair.

"What is it, Whit?"

"You hear about that murder up by Byers' Creek bridge?"

"Yes. Tory Cook."

"I know who did it."

"Go on."

Whit told Pastor Fogel everything about that night up to the point where he saw the three men on the bridge in the rainstorm.

Then he said, "If I tell you who did it, you can't tell anyone what I told you, right?" Whit's hands were massaging each other. He glanced up.

"That's right."

"Hacker Merrone and Buford Butz killed Tory Cook. They beat him and stabbed him in the body and cut his throat. Then they threw him into the creek and left. You familiar with that place?"

"No, Whit." The pastor took a deep breath, held it, let it out. "Thank you for telling me. So, what are you going to do?"

"Merrone and Butz are bad men, always coming after me. But if I testify to what I saw, they'll get off if their lawyer's any good. Then they'll really come after me. They already did that once."

"What happened?"

Whit told the preacher about the dogs.

"It's okay to be afraid of what they'd try to do to you," he said. "That's just sensible."

"I'm not afraid of what they'd try to do to me, Pastor. I'm afraid of what I'd do to *them*."

It was quiet for a time. Then Fogel asked, "Do you have a wife, family, good friend to come alongside you?"

Whit shook his head. "I keep to myself."

Pastor Fogel nodded. "Are you saying if you testify against them and nothing comes of it, you're afraid you'll have to kill them because they'll come after you for testifying?"

"Yes. So I just want to know if I should make a statement to the sheriff."

Jimmy Fogel smiled a rueful smile. Then he said, "You know those bracelets people wore a good while back with 'WWJD' on them?"

"Sure," Whit said. "What Would Jesus Do."

"Right, well, in this case, in *all* cases, we really need to ask that question, as you are. God's word tells us, plain as day, that we need to walk humbly with God and do justice, among other things." Pastor Fogel shrugged and held out his hands, palms up.

"That's what I'm supposed to do in this case?" Whit asked. "What does it mean by 'justice'?"

"I believe justice means putting things right. And we all know what's right, deep down, whether we want to admit it or not, especially when it's inconvenient."

Whit stood. The pastor did as well. Whit said, "What would *you* do, Pastor? Should I go to the sheriff and turn them in?"

"Pray for wisdom. Set things right. You'll know what to do."

"Go see the sheriff?"

"If you believe that will be setting things right, go ahead and tell him."

"Her."

"Tell *her* what you saw. The rest is up to her, up to those men. But you would be wise to be vigilant, given what you said about those two men, and keep your powder dry no matter what you decide."

"Appreciate it."

Whit and the pastor left the building and stopped out in the yard. A hawk screeched in the sky above them, rising on a thermal, circling and circling.

"One more thing, Whit, and I hope it's helpful."

"What's that?"

"This: God loves your enemies as much as He loves you. Tough one, right?"

Whit rolled his shoulders and looked at Pastor Fogel. "I never thought of it that way," he said. "Kind of throws me off a bit."

"Me too," Fogel said.

"You say things that ring true but are pretty hard to swallow, Pastor."

Fogel laughed. "My job. But so's cleaning up this yard. Come back anytime, Whit. You'll always be welcome. I'll pray for you and your situation. Today and tonight and straight on."

"I was gonna ask you to do that."

The men shook hands.

Pastor Fogel said, "You keep in touch, Whit."

Whit nodded and strode over to his pickup truck, started the engine, and left. The two men gained eye contact as Whit pulled out onto the blacktop, and they nodded to each other.

Whit drove straight home, his mind thrashing about from the pastor's words, knowing they were true. No point in praying about it. He mulled their conversation over and over in his mind on the way home. When he pulled onto the graveled area at his cabin, Whit had made his peace.

Inside, his dog approached, wiggling and happy to see him. He thumped Barney on the shoulder and said, "Alright then." That night, he had a big glass of pinot noir, went to bed, and enjoyed a restful sleep.

And the next morning, after his prayer and a big breakfast, he left to go see Sheriff Render.

CHAPTER 15

"Fear doesn't shut you down; it wakes you up."
—Veronica Roth, *Divergent*

THE SHERIFF'S DEPARTMENT of Ransom County was housed in a small brick building with offices at ground level and a jail underneath in a daylight basement. The exterior of the building was decorated with flower beds and a green trash can, an empty bicycle rack, and two sugar maple trees now tinged with orange leaves.

Whit parked his truck next to a patrol car in the four-vehicle parking lot. He got out and walked inside.

A deputy at the front desk looked up from his computer and asked, "Can I help you?" The man's uniform appeared clean and recently pressed. He was built short and square, with a GI haircut, wire-rimmed glasses, and a trim moustache.

"I'm Whit Coombs, and I'm looking for Sheriff Render."

The man stood and said, "I'm Deputy Mason Hipp. What's the nature of your visit?"

"I want to tell her something."

Deputy Hipp paused for a moment, then came out from behind his desk. Whit noticed the Marine Corps eagle, globe, and anchor tattoo on Hipp's right forearm. He also noticed the Glock 9 holstered at his right hip.

"Follow me, sir," Hipp said.

Whit followed the man down a short hall, where the deputy stopped by the second door on the right and rapped three times, military style, on the doorjamb.

Whit heard Sheriff Render say, "Yes, Deputy," and then Hipp announcing Whit's presence. A chair creaked. Hipp turned, eyed Whit, and headed back to his desk.

Sheriff Render presented herself at the door and smiled. Whit noticed again her intense gray eyes as she stepped back and gestured for him to come in and sit down. She closed the door. After she sat back at her desk, he took a seat across from her.

"What can I do for you, Mr. Coombs?"

"Just listen to me."

She cocked her head and raised her eyebrows. She said nothing and waited.

"I saw Merrone and Butz murder Tory Cook that night a while back," Whit said.

Sheriff Render leaned forward. Her chair creaked again. She placed her elbows on the desk, locked in eye contact with Whit, and nodded. "Continue," she said.

Whit gave the details of what he had seen. He sat back when he finished. "Do I need to sign anything?"

"First," she said, "I want to thank you for doing the right thing. I'm glad you came forward. Second, I'd like for you to write and sign a statement reflecting what you just told me. Give the date and approximate time. After you sign your statement, I'll take it from there."

"Are you going to arrest them?"

"Yes."

"Today?"

"Yes, I will be heading out shortly."

"So, you can do that just from what I told you?"

"Yes, I now have probable cause. I believe your story. And I want you to know that I appreciate this."

Whit looked around the sheriff's office. There were several plaques recognizing her contributions to the county. A few framed photographs of her with people Whit did not recognize, certificates from various training academies, a bachelor of science degree from Appalachian State University in Boone. He turned his gaze back to her. She was still focused on him.

"If you find and arrest them, what happens next?" he asked.

She took a deep breath and leaned back into her squeaky chair. Still intense, she showed a hint of a smile.

"I'll lock them up. They'll probably make bail in the morning, which will likely be set at fifty thousand dollars due to the seriousness of the charge: first-degree murder. If they can come up with a ten percent bond, they'll be released. I don't think they're a flight risk. I'm guessing they don't have passports."

Whit nodded. He said, "I would also like to file a complaint based on their coming out to my home and setting those dogs on me. I told you about that."

"I will be happy to add that to the other charges."

"They also cussed me, but I'll let that go," he said.

"You are a forgiving man."

"What else happens now?"

"I'll take this to the district attorney and see if he wants to take the evidence and convene a grand jury. The grand jury will decide on whether Merrone and Butz should be indicted."

"This does not put my mind at ease," Whit said.

"Why is that?"

"I've heard it said that a grand jury can indict a ham sandwich. That it doesn't mean much."

"I've heard that, too," she said. "But it's an important step. If they do indict, and I believe they will since they have not only visual identification, but voice identification, and you're obviously not a raving lunatic—"

"As far as you know," he interrupted.

She smiled and continued, "As far as I know, you're not; you seem like a highly credible witness."

"What can Merrone and Butz do when they get out on bail? Can they come visit me and thank me for doing the right thing?" he asked, thinking back to his conversation with Pastor Fogel.

"They can be ordered to stay away from you."

"So they'll probably obey the order, since they are upright citizens."

"I would take precautions. . . "

"Anything else?" Whit asked, preparing to stand.

"Mr. Coombs, not only do I believe you, but I *know* Merrone and Butz murdered Tory Cook that night up on Byers' Creek," she said. "I have a witness who overheard them bragging about it at a pig roast a while back. Said they were glad they did in Tory Cook, that he needed killing."

"So that gives you two witnesses. Looking better."

"Still one witness. He won't testify. He's afraid to. He's a kid I gave a break a while back over some minor marijuana transactions. I told him not to do it again, and as far as I know, he hasn't. But he still has one foot in that environment and another close to me," she said, coming to her feet, chair squeaking. "For now, I'm going to go look for our friends and lock them up. Then I'll go talk to Hoot and see what he thinks."

"Hoot?"

"Hoot Rider is the DA," she said.

"The DA's name is Hoot?" Whit asked, standing.

"Don't let the nickname fool you. Christian name is Calvin. He's tough and fair, and has a stellar conviction record. He tells funny stories, so that's where he got 'Hoot.'"

"You said 'stellar.' That proves you went to college." Whit glanced back up at the framed diploma on the wall.

"Yes. What about you? College?"

"Some."

"Well, I need to depart," Render said. "Please fill out your statements on the murder and the dog attack and give that information to Deputy

Hipp. I'll be on my way. I'll stop by and let you know how things are progressing. And thanks again, Mr. Coombs."

"I guess you can call me Whit."

"And you can call me Della, when there's just the two of us," she said, smiling.

With that, she left, and Whit sat back down to write his statements.

That evening, in the midst of an intense red and magenta sunset mirrored on the lake, and a good chill in the air, Sheriff Render dropped by the cabin. Whit heard her coming and went outside with Barney. She emerged from her car and approached.

"I've arrested and jailed J. D. Merrone and Buford Butz, but I don't think they'll be in lockup more than just tonight. They didn't have enough cash to make bail, and they couldn't get in touch with a bail bondsman in Asheville, but Merrone has a good bit of land he can put up for collateral. If they take off, he'll lose the land, so I doubt either one of them will disappear. That's all I've got for you so far," she said. "I think they know you're the witness, so be alert. You can sleep tight tonight, though, Whit. I'll keep you posted."

"They got a lawyer, Sheriff? Della."

"Assigned a public defender."

"Any good?"

"Joel Huff. Smart guy, but his experience is mostly with real estate, wills and trusts, general law practice. Chapel Hill Law. He has defended before and did well. I trust him to do his duty to the best of his ability. He might come out to interview you, so be prepared."

"Can he do that? Wouldn't that be an attempt at intimidation?"

"Perfectly legal. You don't have to talk to him if you don't want to," she said. "Anything else, Whit?"

"No. Thanks for the update . . . Della."

Sheriff Render gave Barney a good ears rubbing, turned, got in her car, and left, headlights shining on the changing foliage. When the taillights disappeared around a corner, Whit stopped looking.

Inside, Barney curled up on the love seat, and Whit fixed himself dinner, cleaned up, and read a book in his recliner until he grew sleepy. When he dropped the book a second time, he went to bed.

CHAPTER 16

"Fate loves the fearless."
—James Russell Lowell

TWO MORE DAYS HAD PASSED since the arrest of Hacker Merrone and Buford Butz. Whit strolled down his dirt lane in the morning and was peering into his mailbox when he heard a familiar, distant sound—a pickup truck approaching on Panther Scream Road.

He did not look up. His disability check had arrived, along with a handwritten note. He did not recognize the writer's handwriting as he withdrew the two pieces of mail, his haul for the week. He didn't recognize the nameless return address, either, but it was a woman's handwriting.

Shortly, the truck loomed up, tires chirping as it skidded to a stop just short of running Whit over. He heard one door open and slam shut, and another. Finally, he glanced up and saw what he expected: two angry men.

"You sonuvabitch," Hacker Merrone said, "I ought to cut you up in little pieces and leave you to rot at the side of the road."

The man's face was red, his body rigid, his ponderous fists tight at his sides.

Whit glanced back down at his mail, trying to figure out the source of the note. He guessed he'd go ahead and open it and see.

"Did you hear me, asshole?" Merrone said.

Whit did not answer. He slipped his finger into the fold of the envelope, tore it open, and withdrew the note. He adjusted his glasses. *Nice penmanship.*

"Let's just kill this piece of shit," Butz said. The two men stepped closer, and Whit lifted his gaze, then reached around behind his loose blue sweatshirt, withdrew his revolver, and pointed it at Merrone's forehead.

"Go away," he said. "I'm busy."

"You got us arrested! Put us in jail!" Butz said. "We don't take kindly to that, and you're gonna be so fucking sorry you'll wish you was never born!"

Whit gazed at Butz. "Uh-huh."

"You're lucky you got that pistol in your hand," Merrone said.

"Uh-huh," Whit said.

"If you didn't, we'd be all over your sorry ass," Merrone continued.

"I told you once before. Now leave me alone," Whit said.

"You ain't from aroun' here," Merrone said, "'cuz if you was, you'd know you don't fuck with Buford Butz and J. D. Merrone. Nobody does. You gonna regret goin' to the sheriff."

A chill wind blustered up and around, scattering a few vivid leaves into little orange-and-red tornados. Whit looked up at the cobalt-blue sky, cloudless and autumnal with the day pushing deeper into fall. He didn't want to shoot the men. It would be easy, though. Such target-friendly buffoons. But that would invite scrutiny.

Butz took a step toward Whit, who quickly brought the barrel of the revolver across the bridge of the little man's nose, breaking it. A gush of blood shot forth, and Butz backed away, then fell to his knees, moaning, blood streaming down his face and through his fingers as he took in his injury. Merrone watched his companion fall, and when he looked back at Whit, the barrel of the revolver loomed two inches from his left eye. There was blood splatter on the barrel.

Whit gave a short, strong push, and the barrel jammed hard into Merrone's eye. He yelped in pain and quickly brought his hands to his face, staggering back toward the truck. He bumped into the hood of the decrepit vehicle and lost his balance, slithering to the ground. A torrent of profanity burst from Hacker's mouth even as Butz dragged himself over to the truck and crawled into the passenger's side and shut the door.

"Go away," Whit said. "And stay away."

Merrone muttered more obscenities and stumbled back inside the truck, slamming the door. With his left eye squinched shut, he revved the engine and backed up, both hands on the wheel. Whit wondered if Hacker would try to run him over, and he knew if that happened, he would shoot the man. He was glad when it was clear he would not have to fire his revolver.

Whit watched the truck make a U-turn on Screaming Panther Road and roar away to the north, toward town. His glance took in several red and sugar maples with their fiery colors coming on full bore now. He liked the thought of leaves dying and sacrificing all that living color on their way to barrenness, giving deeper value to their beauty.

When the truck was gone, he tucked the handgun under his sweatshirt and into the back of his blue jeans. Then he opened the note and saw that it was a thank-you from the artist lady, Bev.

He stuffed the empty, torn envelope in his back pocket and walked the three miles back to his cabin, reading the note two times. It was a nice note, and a wish for his well-being. It ended with, *And perhaps, Whit, we might meet again and talk about art. Please bring Barney.*

She signed it, *As always, Bev.*

A postscript read, *I'll be showing my work again at the Oktoberfest in Mitchum City on October 2-4. Hope you'll stop by and say hello.*

Back inside his cabin, Whit rubbed Barney's ears and the spot where the tail connected to the butt. A dreamy look came over the big dog's face, and he licked his chops. Whit laughed and gave Barney a Milk Bone just because he could. Then he cleaned the blood splatter from his revolver and set it on the kitchen counter.

He was hungry, and so he put together a lunch for himself. Shredded ham and extra sharp cheddar cheese between two slices of whole wheat bread was a good start. He still had a couple of slices of a store-bought peach pie in a tin, so he put those on the table along with the sandwich. He poured a glass of whole milk and sat down and thought about Beverly Andreeson.

He wondered where she was from. Her family, her friends. Where she lived. What else she did besides paint beautiful landscapes. He ate his lunch while he thought about her, gave Barney the last bite from his sandwich, ate both pieces of pie, and set the empty tin on the floor for his dog to clean up.

He exited the back door, leaving Barney inside, when he heard a car crunching on the gravel in his parking area. Whit shook his head and muttered. He walked around the side of the house and saw a Ransom County Sheriff's Department cruiser pulling to a stop. The door on the driver's side opened and Sheriff Render stepped out. Her hair was a bit disheveled, and her uniform blouse was not completely tucked in. She had traded shorts for slacks. Colder weather, especially after dark. She strode toward the cabin, Whit ambled toward the sheriff, and they met about halfway.

"Hello, Della."

"I can't believe you did it," she said, her voice terse.

He cocked his head in question, even though he knew.

"I just came from a quick meeting with J. D. Merrone and Buford Butz. They look like hell. Butz's shirtfront is covered with blood and his nose has a little dip in the middle where you broke it. And Merrone's left eye looks like a cherry tomato!"

Whit chuckled.

"It's not funny, Whit! They're saying you went after them, and this will come up in court when the defense lawyer makes it look like you're just after these two, and trying to frame them. They swore out a complaint against you. We took pictures!"

"I thought they were ordered to stay away from me."

"They were!"

"So what were they doing out here?"

"They said they came out to apologize about the dogs."

Whit shook his head and smiled, the unexpected expression making him look like a different person. She started to laugh. Quickly, she caught herself and forced a glare at Whit, but it was spurious, and he knew it. He smiled again.

"Whit, that was still wrong to beat them up. It won't look good in court."

"I'll take my chances."

"Do you want to file a complaint against them coming out here? Might help your case. Can't hurt," she said.

"Okay. Tomorrow, alright?"

Sheriff Render sighed and shook her head and said, "You're a real piece of work, Whit."

He just smiled again.

Render turned, hastened toward her patrol car, and got in. She spun a bit of gravel as she left the parking area behind.

Whit returned to the back of his cabin to let Barney out and grab a paddle, and strode out to the dock where he launched his red cedar canoe. Barney flopped down on the deck. Whit glided softly onto the placid blue lake, now reflecting not only the Blue Ridge in the short distance, but the vivid colors of the trees around the lake.

Whit loved autumn.

CHAPTER 17

"It is justice, not charity, that is
wanting in this world."
—Mary Wollstonecraft

WHIT DROVE INTO TOWN MIDMORNING and filed his complaint against J. D. Merrone and Buford Butz. Sheriff Render was not in. A deputy sheriff stationed at the front desk handled the process after quickly standing and introducing himself as Deputy Drew Poteet. The man was tall, lanky, and blond, and exuded military bearing, a reflection of his boss. When Whit finished his paperwork, he handed it over and started for the door.

"You done good, Mister Coombs," the man said. Whit nodded and left.

The cold air from the night before lingered on into the morning. Whit had slipped on a long-sleeved denim shirt over his T-shirt. The added cover felt good, the shirt being old and worn and as comfortable as a compliment.

So, with a rich September day ahead of him, he drove home and gathered up Barney and headed for Hastings Corners. Time to gas up and go see what the day had in store. The short drive through the thick woods settled Whit after his few minutes in the Ransom County Sheriff's Department and his disappointment at not being able to see Sheriff Render. He wondered where she was as he pulled into Homer's Gas & Groceries.

The double gas pump was occupied by a white, four-door pickup truck. The back window had decals for Harley-Davidson and the NRA. A bumper sticker proclaimed, *You've seen the mountains, now get the hell back to Florida.* The driver was leaning against his truck, thick arms folded across a burly chest, letting the pump run itself. A green baseball cap barely contained a thicket of brown hair. A rough beard covered his benign face.

The pump clicked off. The man replaced the handle, took his receipt, and drove away into the sunlight and shadows. Whit pulled forward and filled up before heading inside.

Homer was stocking the cigarette display behind the counter. He looked up and said, "Mornin', Whit. Didja see where your ol' buddies got locked up, leastways for a bit?"

Whit continued on into the store.

"Yeah," Homer went on, "they been charged in that Tory Cook killin'. I gotta hand it to Sheriff Render, man. She bein' no bigger'n a bad opinion and goin' up on the mountain and bringin' those boys in by herself. Girl's got gumption, that one."

"So I hear," Whit said, placing a Banana Flip, a package of Zingers, and an individual Krispy Kreme fried apple pie in his shopping basket. With his free hand, he snagged a twelve-pack of Heineken and stepped up to Homer.

The store owner rang up the purchases, saying, "I guess you aren't heartbroken about those boys gettin' busted, way Hacker went after Barney that day."

"I pumped 37.65 of regular," Whit said.

Homer bagged up the food in a limp plastic bag and slid it over to Whit, and said, "You think they'll get sent off?"

"We'll see."

"Well, I don't guess there'll be too many tears around here if they live the rest of their lives in Marion," Homer said, taking the bills and change for the exact amount. "You have a good day, now, y'hear?"

"You too."

Whit strode outside and climbed into his truck and opened the package of yellow Zingers, gave one to Barney, ate another as they sat together in the cab. The big dog's stitched ear was healing well, and the few puncture wounds in his neck's loose skin were nearly invisible. Whit rubbed his dog's sholders, always impressed with the rock-hard muscle tone. He gave Barney an affectionate pat.

What began as a pleasant trip into the village had been marred by Homer bringing up the murder and arrests. Whit finished his second Zinger and placed the trash back in the bag. He started the engine, pulled away, and headed back toward home.

On the way, it occurred to Whit that he had not gone for a hike in days. The fact surprised him. Too many conversations interrupting his life, and then the run-in with Hacker and Butz.

"That explains it," he said out loud, looking over at Barney. "Hey, boy, wanna go for a walk?"

Barney rose from his sitting position, edged across the console, and slurped Whit's face. Whit laughed in spite of himself as his dog, tail wagging with enthusiasm, regained his position back in the shotgun seat.

When they pulled off Panther Scream Road and eased down the three miles of dirt to the cabin, Whit felt gratitude for the place where he lived and the life that he led, and he was confident that a healthy hike was all he needed to get his bearings back. He knew he had nothing to fear. Hacker and Butz fell short of the kinds of enemies Whit had taken on in the military. He just didn't want to be bothered.

Inside the cabin, Whit changed into his old hiking boots and gathered up his equipment (handgun, canteen, energy bars, knife) and started out. The man and his dog took a different path than usual, one they had not taken in a year or so—south into the mountains rather than their usual north and west hikes. The trail offered steeper and longer climbs, but Whit welcomed the challenge, looking forward to working up a cleansing sweat.

Barney eagerly swung into a steady pace, ranging after an occasional squirrel and taking off after a rabbit. Whit smiled at his dog's enthusiasm for the chase, even though his tormentors cheated. Squirrels scampered up trees, and rabbits would not run in a straight line. Once, a year or two back, Barney had caught a squirrel, but instead of killing it, he had just prodded it with his nose to make the squirrel run faster.

Whit smiled at the memory.

When Whit and Barney returned from their hike they noticed a man sitting in his car in the gravel in front of the cabin. He emerged as Whit and Barney approached.

"I'm Joel Huff," he said, walking up to Whit and offering his hand.

"I figured," Whit said, shaking hands.

"Are you Whit Coombs?"

"I am."

"Nice dog you got there, Whit. Okay to pet him?" He extended his hand.

"Sure."

Huff patted Barney on the head while the big dog provided a cursory sniffing of the man's hand before sitting down next to Whit. Huff then pulled back and straightened up, brushing his hand against his leg. He wore khaki pants, a long-sleeved blue dress shirt, and a red tie. And blue Nikes.

"I'm the public defender for J. D. Merrone and Buford Butz."

"I know."

"Mind if we go inside and have a chat?"

"I do mind if we go inside. People shouldn't invite themselves into someone else's home. It's the other way around."

Huff smiled and stuffed his hands inside his pockets. Whit expected the man to kick at the white gravel a little with his Nikes. Then he did exactly that. *Folksy.*

"Nice place you have here," Huff said, glancing around. "Hard to find, but I guess that's the point, isn't it?"

Whit said nothing while maintaining eye contact.

"I thought we could talk a little bit about what you allegedly saw the other night a while back, when you claim you saw my clients murder Tory Cook. Of course, if you don't want to, you aren't compelled to."

"We agree on that."

"I see you're wearing glasses. Could you tell me a little about your vision issues? Any hearing issues?"

"No."

Huff smiled and pulled his hands out of his pockets, kicked a little more at the gravel, held out his hand to shake. Whit did not return the gesture.

"We already shook." Whit started to say he was sorry Huff drove out for nothing but decided not to. Waste of words. Also a lie. He was pleased that the man had made a fruitless trip.

"I guess the saying is 'See you in court,' which I will. Good day," Huff said. He climbed into his white Acura and left.

"Let's get something to eat, boy," Whit said to Barney, and they headed for the cabin. They had just reached the front porch when another car emerged from the trees.

"Shit," Whit muttered. Someone else interrupting his solitude. *Damn parade of people.* Then he realized the car was a Ransom County Sheriff cruiser. He stepped down from the porch after letting Barney inside and walked toward the car.

Della Render exited her cruiser and approached the cabin. Whit met her halfway, noticing that she looked a little tired around the eyes, but her uniform was crisp, and her short blonde hair looked nice.

"I have good news and bad news, Whit."

"Go ahead."

"Which first?"

He tilted his head a little and raised his eyebrows.

"No," she said. "You're right. No games. Good news is that we're taking Merrone and Butz to court for trial. Bad news is the date is set for February 15."

"That's five months from now," Whit said with a hint of annoyance. He calmed himself and said in a normal voice, "Long time."

"I agree, but actually, that's relatively quick. Trials usually take place six to twelve months down the line after an arrest. Not many cases waiting to be heard around here, though. Both lawyers agreed to move it up a little bit. Still, I'm sorry," she said, shifting her weight from one foot to the other.

"It's okay," he said. "Joel Huff just left."

"I met him on my way out here. Figured."

"I told him I didn't want to talk."

"Figured that, too."

"So, what should I do for the next five months?"

"Go about your life. They won't do anything to jeopardize their standing. I don't think they cared much for being in jail," she said.

"Jimmy Fogel told me to keep my powder dry."

"Jimmy Fogel?"

"Pastor at God's Grace Church."

"Oh, well, not a bad idea. We can step up patrols out this way in the duration," she said, folding her arms.

"I can take care of myself."

"I'm starting to believe you, Whit."

He wanted to ask her in. He wanted to say, casually, "Della, would you like to come in for a minute? I could get you a beer. Heineken. In a glass." But he knew she would say no. After all, she was on duty.

She said, "Are you okay, Whit?"

"I'm fine. Why?"

"I don't know. Your expression changed, like you were worried."

"I'm fine," he repeated.

"I'll be around. Call me if anything comes up, okay?"

"I will."

"Well, then. . . " she said. Still, she just stood there. He expected her to leave, but she remained in place. It was quiet for a few moments.

"Well," she said again, dropping her arms to her side, flapping her hands against her thighs, "gotta go."

"Okay, Della. Appreciate the heads-up."

He watched her walk to the cruiser, enjoying how she moved. *Vital.* She got in, started up the engine, waved at him through the windshield. He waved back. She turned around and headed out. He watched until she disappeared around a copse of gold-leafed sugar maples.

Whit's stomach growled as he ascended the front porch and entered the cabin. Barney slid off a sofa and came to him, wagging his tail, his broad face happy. After dinner, Whit poured himself a big glass of red wine, picked up a novel, and settled into his recliner.

An hour later he set aside his reading and stood, pacing and thinking about the five months he had to wait before Merrone and Butz, and himself, would be in the courtroom. And he berated himself over his lack of initiative with Della, not even giving her a chance to decline an invitation to join him for a beer inside the cabin.

He stepped out on the back porch with Barney and just looked at the lake and the sky and took in the chill night air of the coming season. Then he released his frustration, a soft supplication for patience taking it away.

A few minutes later, he went to bed and soon fell asleep, grateful for the resumed quiet that surrounded his life and his cabin, and the peace as gentle and deep and soft as a penitent's prayer.

CHAPTER 17

"Fear's useless. Either something bad happens or
it doesn't: If it doesn't, you've wasted time being afraid,
and if it does, you've wasted time that you could've
been sharpening your weapons."
—Sarah Rees Brennan, *The Demon's Lexicon*

HIS REFLEXES SAVED HIM when the timber rattler struck inches
from his face after he opened up his mailbox. He jumped back as the broad
head, curved fangs, and pink mouth fell to the ground where the snake's
momentum had carried it, pulled out his .38, and shot it three times.

"I hate snakes," he said out loud.

Barney had darted away, startled by the gunshots, but now came back
slowly, eyes locked on the serpent on the ground. The big dog stretched
his head far ahead of his feet, leaning forward cautiously, and sniffed the
dead serpent. Then he stepped back and looked at Whit.

"Come 'ere, Barney.

Barney slunk to Whit's side, where his master stroked him along his
back and rubbed his ears. Barney wagged his tail but kept his eyes on

the dead snake. Whit prodded the rattler with his foot, lengthening it out, aware that "dead" snakes have been known to bite. But this snake no longer had a head. The reptile was nearly six feet long and as thick as Whit's forearm. Six rattles. The distinctive dark cross-bands over a mottled gray background looked like chevrons. He picked it up by the black tail and slung it into the underbrush on the side of his dirt lane. It had heft.

Whit looked inside his mailbox again. Nothing else there. He turned and walked back up the dirt lane leading to his cabin, following Barney, who ranged ahead a few yards, looking over his shoulder from time to time to be sure Whit was coming along. Whit laughed at the big dog's expression as they walked.

"Snakes can be bad, Barney," he said. Barney's tail swept back and forth as he trotted along, acting more like himself the farther they left the snake behind.

Whit glanced around at the trees on his property, with a new appreciation for the beauty of the seasons, and life itself, since he had avoided a potentially lethal snakebite. A wide range of color surrounded him—red from red maples and sassafras trees, gold from sugar maples and poplars, and orange from American beech trees.

Of course, it wouldn't last. Nothing that spectacular could, not in the real world, but Whit had learned over the years and the seasons that beauty needed to be taken in when possible, and let go when that time came. He could not make it stay. All he could do was be thankful.

Back at the cabin, Whit reloaded his .38 and chastised himself for wasting three rounds on the rattler. Emotional reaction to a threat—not how he'd been trained. On the other hand, he cut himself some slack. He had never been trained to respond to a deadly snake in his mailbox. A gap in Army training.

"I'm just glad I didn't soil myself, Barney," he said. Barney wagged his tail.

Whit refused to let the incident ruin his love for the season. He kept taking long walks in the mountains with his dog and silent paddles into the blue lake's still waters, and viewing an occasional college football game on TV. And so September slipped away into October with no more contact from Merrone or Butz. Whit had not reported the snake incident. There was no point.

He wrestled with the idea of attending the Mitchum County Oktoberfest every time he reread Beverly Andreeson's handwritten note. The more he thought about it, the more he came to believe that maybe she was interested in him. The thought was pleasing. Acting on it was intimidating. Why start something he could never finish? Why toy with her emotions, if indeed she was interested? What if he didn't buy any more of her paintings? Was her interest just good business?

He decided to go see her again. Friday, the first day of the Oktoberfest, dawned sunny with an azure sky and whipped-cream clouds piled high like hopes at a wedding. Whit rose from his bed, prayed his prayer, pulled on sweats. He fixed breakfast for Barney but none for himself. He was distracted, and not hungry as a result. He showered, shaved off a few days' worth of whiskers, and walked out to the end of the dock. He took in a deep breath of nippy air, exhaled. He was hoping it would be cold enough to see his breath, but it was too soon.

He called Barney and they entered the cabin together. Whit tried on both of his sweaters twice each before settling on the blue one. Then he took off that sweater, thinking maybe Beverly would like more contrast in his attire, she being an artist and all. So he finally slipped on his red sweater. To go with her hair.

He didn't want to arrive at the Oktoberfest too early. It was 9:30 now, and it would take half an hour to drive into Mitchum. He picked up a book and sat back in his recliner but gave up on it after a few pages and set it in his bookshelf. He reread Beverly's note, just to be sure. Replaced it on the mantel. Balanced his checkbook, which took five minutes because Whit rarely wrote checks. He used the envelope method of keeping cash on hand for purchases he might make. He liked the feel of currency in his hands, the tangibility of the paper. He double-checked each envelope.

An envelope for art didn't exist, so he pirated $250 from several envelopes and folded over the money and stuffed it in his pocket, his budget corrupted but cash now available for another painting, maybe. Something smaller than his previous purchase. He grabbed his keys, his interest in seeing Beverly overcoming his aversion to the push of crowds that nearly made him emetic. He left Barney behind to avoid subjecting him again to rude children. The big dog was curling up on his favorite sofa when Whit left.

He took his time driving into Mitchum, stretching beyond the normal half hour. He arrived and followed *Parking $5* signs to a vacant lot next to a strip mall, grateful for the cheaper parking. Bigger town, more competition, he guessed. Sunburned fat men in camo cargo pants and orange Clemson T-shirts gestured him onto the property, taking his money and waving him on to the next man until Whit had parked and gotten out.

Whit didn't wear a watch, and the clock in the truck was unreliable, but it had to be after eleven, he decided, looking up at the sun as he followed small groups of people headed downtown, two blocks away. He didn't like to pay money for the privilege of parking his truck—it was twice now he'd done that. He guessed he might have to start an envelope marked *Parking* and then smiled at the idea. Maybe one for local art. At least that way there was something he could look at and put his hands on that would last beyond the day he paid for parking.

The festival presented just like the last one, only bigger. The same booths were selling food, wooden yard ornaments (geese in bow ties, ducks, cute skunks), T-shirts with coarse messages next to Christian wisecracks (*Not Today, Satan!*), and handmade jewelry. Whit looked at the jewelry for a few minutes, surprised at the beauty and delicacy of some pieces. He turned down overtures from artists attempting to interest him in their crafts, but he did almost buy a jade pendant on a thin gold chain that would look nice on Beverly, given her coloring. But he fought off that impulse as too forward, too presumptuous, and too expensive, and besides, he wouldn't have enough cash then to perhaps buy another painting. So he strolled deeper into the Oktoberfest, passing a beer tent that was beginning to attract thirsty people. Hamburgers, bratwurst, and waffle fries were also available. Whit's stomach started to churn as he enjoyed the redolent smells from the tent.

And then he saw her.

She was set up on the sidewalk in front of her yellow tent, painting while talking to foot traffic. Whit had seen that kind of thing before, including once in a national park out West where the artist had a sign saying, *Please do not interrupt the artist. She is working.*

Whit had wondered about the artist at the time. If she wanted peace and quiet, why the heck did she make a point of being next to a footpath leading to an overlook?

But this was different. Beverly chatted away while she dabbed paint on a canvas on a sturdy tripod. Whit watched her and was taken in. The sun was shining on her red hair, and it practically glowed, gold flecks scattered throughout. The single braid trailed down her back, a white peasant's blouse providing backdrop to show off her tresses. He admired her appearance from his position behind her, the womanly curves and strong stance. She was talking to a handsome man, laughing together with him, almost intimate in their conversation.

Whit considered turning around and going back, his five bucks wasted, and heading on home. *How foolish to think. . .*

Then he stopped and decided to step up and say hello. Five dollars was a lot of money to throw away, and besides, there might be other attractions to enjoy, or, now that he was hungry, that food frying back at the beer tent.

He ambled over and situated himself to her left and back a little to peer over her shoulder at the street scene she was painting, surprised because all he had seen before were landscapes. And here was a street scene coming to life under her brush, the morning sunlight emphasizing strong colors in the subject. He studied how her hands moved and how she was able to match up colors from her palette with the actual colors before her.

"Your work is going to take off," the man said. "Have a great festival."

The man—Whit's age, maybe younger—looked at Whit and smiled and nodded, then left. She watched him go and, as she turned, caught Whit in her peripheral vision and turned fully to face him.

"Whit!" she said, "how nice to see you! If I'd known you were standing there, I would have introduced you to my agent!"

Whit's relief skipped across his face. Beverly noticed, and smiled. She asked, "What brings you here?"

"Beer," he said. "This is Oktoberfest, right?"

"Tough to beat art and beer," she said, cocking her head and smiling.

"Can I buy you lunch?" he asked before he could stop himself.

"It's about that time, isn't it? Let me see if I can get someone to keep an eye on my work," she said. She flipped a canvas over her painting in progress and turned to an old, skinny, white-haired man working at a booth of hand-carved miniature animals and chess pieces.

"Raymond, would you keep an eye on my paintings, please?" she said.

He said, "Go ahead, Bev. Take your time."

And with that, Whit and Beverly headed for the beer tent as he fought the urge to take her hand in his.

CHAPTER 18

"I will never love you, the cost of love's too dear."
—Gail Garnett, "We'll Sing in the Sunshine"

WALKING WITH BEVERLY back to the beer tent, treading the same steps he had taken as he approached her, observing the same sights and smells that he had found assaultive to his senses and confining to his mind before, didn't seem so bad now. She was with him, and now he felt open to the crowds of people and cacophony of sounds and abundance of fragrances.

A pair of wild boys rapidly approached, racing through the crowd, bumping mindlessly into people. Before they could jar Whit and Beverly, he put out his left hand and placed his right hand on her elbow, moving her a little farther out of the boys' path. The kids veered off into another couple, bouncing away down the street, laughing.

"Nicely done," she said.

Whit dropped his hand from her elbow and nodded, and so they continued on to the beer tent, where a short line awaited. They got in the queue and studied the whiteboard overhead with the handwritten menu items, the fragrance of brats and burgers cooking on a grill, waffle fries bubbling in vats of hot oil prodding customers' appetites.

"I am really hungry, so let's go Dutch," she said, eyes turned upwards, smiling.

"I believe I invited you to lunch, so, no, I've got it," he responded.

"Do you mean to tell me this is a date?"

"I guess."

"Sheesh, I haven't been on a date since Nixon was a boy."

Whit smiled as they moved up to the front of the line, Beverly ordering her beer first, then Whit, both of them going for Blue Moon. A bewhiskered young man in Bermuda shorts, a dark-blue Duke T-shirt, and backwards baseball cap assembled their food order on a red plastic tray, handed it over, and took payment as he smiled and said, "Thank you!" *Nothing like living in the South*, Whit thought. Then he realized he had not prepared to buy food, and now some of his money for a possible painting purchase had eroded.

They each held a flimsy translucent cup of the amber beer. In his other hand Whit carried their tray bearing three bratwursts and two orders of waffle fries. He looked for and found a place with two plastic chairs. The formica table was smeared with faint mustard streaks. Whit put down the tray, set his beer next to it, then seated Bev. He took his seat.

She said, "Thank you, Whit," her voice elevated to combat the multitudinous conversations buzzing around them.

He nodded and allowed himself a small smile. "Your agent seemed friendly."

"He's a decent sort, and if he weren't, I have a dandy left jab."

Whit held up his beer, eliciting the same from her. They touched cups, careful not to slosh. He said, "To Oktoberfest and lots of sold art."

Beverly smiled, and Whit realized again how nice looking she was. Strong features, those green eyes, red hair. A beauty, really.

"I'll drink to that," she said.

"I don't know much about agents, so what does he do for you, besides take ten percent of your earnings?"

"It's fifteen percent these days," she said, "and he really does earn it—not that he's getting rich off me. He has more successful clients to pay his bills." She bit into her bratwurst, rolling her eyes in satisfaction and covering her mouth with one hand. She chewed, swallowed, and said, "But he gets me gigs like this one and handles my social media presence, keeps me alert to other shows and contests."

"So it's worth it."

"I think so. For instance, he got me space in a gallery in Knoxville, and one of my large paintings sold."

"I think all your paintings should sell."

"You're very kind to say so. And generous. Thank you for lunch. I was hungry and thirsty, and bottled water and Oktoberfest do not go together."

Whit dabbed a waffle fry into ketchup he had squeezed onto the waxed paper on their tray. "I went to Oktoberfest in Munich once." He took a bite and chewed.

"Really! What was it like?"

"Big tents put up by breweries, stout women serving one-point-five-liter glass mugs to hundreds of people. Lots of singing. No fights."

"I'll bet you there's at least one fight each day during this Oktoberfest."

"Let's hope not."

"So, where's Barney? I wish you'd brought him. He's such a beautiful, big softy."

"He is that. I just didn't want to risk having some punk try to stab him in the eye again." Whit finished his waffle fry and picked up his half of the third bratwurst they had agreed to split, glad he'd skipped breakfast.

"I thought you both showed patience with that wretched family. And you did well with those boys just now, almost as if you expected trouble," she said. She drank some of her beer.

"Always expect trouble," he said.

"Is that a military thing? Were you in the service?"

"Army."

"How long?"

"Twenty years."

"What did you do in the Army?"

"What I was told."

"Oh," she said, taken aback by his abrupt tone. She looked down.

"That was rude. Sorry," he said softly.

"It's okay. I guess I was a little nosy. Let's change the subject."

"No, you're fine. Go ahead. Ask all the questions you want. But you know. . ."

"If you answer some questions, you'll have to kill me afterwards," she finished, laughing, touching a paper napkin to her mouth. He liked the sound of her laugh. It was hearty and real and contagious. She picked up her half of the third bratwurst. "Okay," she proceeded, "what did you do in the Army? Were you in combat? Did you serve in other countries?" She bit into the sandwich.

"I was a grunt; by that I mean I was in the infantry. Iraq. More combat than I wanted." He turned his head away and roughed up his hair that covered the scar. "That ear doesn't work so well," he said, wishing immediately he had not revealed so much. He didn't need pity.

"What happened with that?"

"RPG. Rocket-propelled grenade from ambush."

"Did you get the guy?"

"Yes, but he got two of us. Friends."

Her face softened as she found herself staring, meeting his eyes. "I'm sorry, Whit," she said. "But did you like the Army?"

"Very much. Clarity of people's position, chain of command, accountability. Decent pay from my perspective. Benefits." He picked up another waffle fry and ate it, with more ketchup.

She looked around as Whit finished his beer and half sandwich. Then she froze, her eyes going wide.

He followed her stare. Buford Butz and Hacker Merrone were standing together at the edge of the beer tent, smirking at some little joke they shared while they eyed her.

"Let's go, Whit. I need to get back to my painting. I don't want to make Ray wait too long. He needs to take lots of potty breaks."

Whit raised an eyebrow, a brief question on his face.

"Ray's eighty-three," she said.

"Oh," Whit said. "Yes, well, we'd better get going."

Whit stood, then helped Beverly from her chair and started out of the tent, Beverly just a half step behind him. Butz and Hacker stood in their way. Beverly seemed to shrink into herself. Whit stepped in front of her and stopped.

"Stand aside," he said.

"Sure thing," Hacker replied, moving out of their path. "Just nice to see a couple of old friends. Both of y'all," he said, bending his head down to get a better look at Beverly. Butz was snickering.

"Oh God, oh God," Beverly whispered to herself.

Whit studied her face. She looked older than she had just moments ago, diminished somehow. He took her hand and helped her along with him, keeping his body between the two men and Beverly as they passed.

"You could at least say something," Hacker said, "or do a snake got your tongue?"

At that, the men laughed and nudged each other. Hacker touched the bill of his baseball cap in mock deference to Beverly, then cooed, "And especially nice seeing you again, ma'am."

"Quickly," she whispered.

Whit led her away, steadily eyeing the two men, who were staring.

"You're still a peach of a girl!" Butz called out.

Beverly twisted loose from Whit's hand, screamed, "SHUT UP!" at the two men, then turned back to Whit, her face pale, her body trembling.

"What's this?" a woman's voice called out. "Stop!"

Sheriff Della Render elbowed her way through a small crowd that had gathered. Whit and Beverly stopped and turned. Buford and Hacker were smirking.

"That there girl cussed me for no reason," Hacker snarled, pointing.

"Me too!" Butz said.

"That's bullshit, boys, and we all know it. I was just standing over there," Sheriff Render said, "and I didn't hear any cussing. Now go on," she said. "Scoot." She made a shooing gesture with her hands.

"Ain't you gonna do nothing about her language assaulting us? We gonna press charges!" Hacker said. "We're victims!"

"That's up to you. But I can file charges against you for not staying clear of Mister Coombs, as ordered by the court. So go ahead, Mister Merrone. Do what you think is best," Render said. "My suggestion is for you to go home, or at least head in the opposite direction of Miz Andreeson and Mister Coombs. And I don't want any more fussin' from any of you. Got it?" She looked around and elicited nodding heads from everyone.

And with that, the gathering of onlookers dispersed. Hacker and Buford headed south, and Beverly and Whit moved north, walking back to her display. When they arrived, she thanked Raymond, offered to return the favor, and flipped the canvas covering free of her easel while the woodcarver scooted away to the closest port-a-potty.

Whit put his hand on her shoulder and asked, "What was that with those two?"

She stopped what she was doing and said, "I don't really want to talk about it."

Whit nodded and said, simply, "Okay." He didn't want to talk about it, either.

CHAPTER 20

"I just want to sleep. A coma would be nice. Or amnesia.
Anything, just to get rid of this, these thoughts, whispers
in my mind. Did he rape my head, too?"
—Laurie Halse Anderson, *Speak*

SHERIFF RENDER HAD FOLLOWED THEM, interrupting Beverly's remarks but not hearing the words, the artist relieved to be free of the topic. Enough had been said.

"You want to tell me what happened back there?" the sheriff asked. Her tone was gentle, her eyes intense. The faint sounds of banjos and "Foggy Mountain Breakdown" wafted across the grounds.

"No," Beverly said, studying her sandals.

"Okay then. Look, those guys are no good, and so I guess you know that, too. Let me know if there's anything I can do, or if you decide to tell me what precipitated that altercation, okay?"

"I will let you know if you can do anything," Beverly said. She looked the sheriff in the eye. "But there isn't."

Render shrugged and turned away. "If you say so. Y'all have a good one, now, y' hear?" And she melted into the crowd and was gone.

Beverly began gathering up her display. Raymond returned and thanked her for watching his miniatures.

"If you'd like to go get something to eat, we can cover for you. Happy to do it," she said to the old man.

He said, "No, but thanks" and turned to his work, smiling.

It was quiet then as Beverly busied herself with collecting her materials. Whit did not know what to say, so he said nothing. He stood next to her in silence.

"I think I'll call it a day," she said.

Whit reached out and stopped her and covered her hands with his. It felt unnatural and forced to him, but he didn't know what else to do without words. As his hands closed on hers, she dropped her chin to her chest, avoiding his eyes. He noticed that she smelled nice, standing that close to him.

He remembered Susan doing the same thing when she was upset, looking down when she first heard her diagnosis. It seemed to help, but later she told him how much she needed for him to look her in the eye and talk about it. When he didn't know how to, she began shutting him out, and it was only later that he realized his mistake might have been the beginning of the erosion of their marriage, their love for each other, their trust, shattered by his clumsiness.

He took a chance. He said, "It's going to be alright."

She looked up at him and said, "No, Whit, it is never going to be alright. It will never be okay."

"Then maybe it will at least get better, after a while."

"It has gotten better," she said, turning away, "but it will never go away. It's there every single day."

It was then that Whit finally understood. "I didn't mean what happened to you would be okay, just that, right now, with me. . . " He stopped talking.

"What do you mean?"

"Never mind," he said. "I don't know. I'm just really sorry about what happened to you, with those two."

"I think I'll finish packing up and go home. I am very tired."

"How long ago did it happen?" he asked, tentative.

"Whit, do you remember the day when you were injured?" she asked.

"Oh."

"'Oh' indeed," she said.

"I don't remember getting blown up, just the effects."

"I remember everything."

"Let me help you," he said suddenly. He could at least be useful, if not comforting. He fumbled in his head, desperate for the right words, haunted by Susan.

"If you want," Beverly said.

He nodded and began folding up easels and carefully loading canvases into her Honda SUV. He took down her yellow tent and put it in her vehicle, all this in silence.

When she was ready to go, he opened the door for her. She climbed in, put her foot on the brake, and pressed a button. The engine came to life. He pushed the door shut. She looked down at the steering wheel for a moment, gathering her thoughts, then turned and met Whit's eyes through the open window. His face was mournful and honest, downcast and transparent.

"Tell me, Whit, what did the sheriff mean back there? Court-ordered restraining order?"

"Yes."

"What about it?"

"I'm going to testify to something I saw them do a while back."

"Good for you," she said. "Was it pretty bad, what you saw?"

"Yes."

She turned back to her right and retrieved one of her business cards and a pen from the console. On the blank side of the card, she wrote down her address and home phone number. She put the pen back and stared at the card while Whit stood silently. Finally, she sighed and turned to Whit and handed him her card.

"I already have one of those. It's on my mantel," he said, "under your painting."

"Turn it over."

He turned over the card and looked back at her, confused.

"That's where I live and that's my cell phone. I think I might like to see you again, Whit. Sometime. We just might have something in common, and what an irony if it's those two creeps."

"But I messed up," he said. "I keep saying the wrong things. Stupid."

"I don't think you're stupid. You're too hard on yourself, but, Whit, you are so straightforward and kind, I don't know whether to laugh or cry. So maybe more time together will help me decide which I should do."

"My words came out all wrong, and I made it worse."

"Only a little," she said. Then she forced a smile and put her foot on the brake and shifted to reverse. The little backup camera showed her the way out.

"I liked the way you yelled at them," he said. "But. . . "

"But?"

"I would've liked to have seen your left jab."

She smiled and took her foot off the brake, backed into an open space, shifted into drive and drove off, her eye on the congested traffic. When she was clear, she glanced in the rearview mirror through her tears and saw Whit standing alone in the road, watching her leave.

CHAPTER 20

"Our doubts are traitors and make us lose the good
we oft might win by fearing to attempt."
—William Shakespeare

TWO MONTHS PASSED as October shuffled off into the past, leaving a trail of dead leaves, and November, then December, rolled into the woods and mountains behind two big snowstorms that smoothed out the land and softened sound like layers of white insulation.

Whit liked the winter—the bleak beauty of it, how the branches of the trees were exposed, their stark silhouettes against the white backdrop of the snow and brittle blue of the sky, mirroring their own root systems below the frozen ground.

He had put his garden to rest, finished stocking up on wood for the following winter, his current supply seasoned from the previous year, and made two trips to Mitchum City where he took advantage of a Walmart to resupply his pantry in case he was snowbound for a few days, which happened sometimes.

And, of course, he and Barney took their almost-daily hikes into the mountains and around the lake, Barney joyfully sniffing the various animal tracks imprinted in the snow like hieroglyphics. Whit had identified rabbit and squirrel, coyote and fox, bear, and on the far side of the lake, a great distance from his cabin, the big prints of a cougar. The lake itself was frozen around the edges, shelves of ice circling the open water like a bib, strong enough to walk on a little way out before the walker's weight made the ice creak and groan with fair warning.

Christmas came and went. Sheriff Render stopped by the cabin and presented a fruitcake to Whit, who was reading a gardening book he had given himself for the holiday. He fetched a fine bottle of pinot noir he had been saving and gave it to her in return. She accepted the wine but declined his invitation to share the fruitcake, then continued on her patrols.

Sometimes that midwinter, Whit and Barney would take a nighttime hike, the snow on the land glittering and blue and silent. On the occasion of two snowstorms, they had even hiked a couple of miles into the mountains during the storms themselves, feasting on the added privacy of no one else being out and about, enjoying the pure, lonely solitude. And once a week, on Thursday, they would walk to the mailbox and retrieve the odd pieces of junk mail, a bill or two, and the two Army checks.

A few weeks after his "date" with Beverly, it occurred to Whit that he should give her a call, that maybe things had calmed down a little for her, even though he detested telephone conversations. On his way home from the Oktoberfest he had cursed himself for being so dumb with her, so ham-handed and dull. Now, he was willing to risk contact again.

He didn't know what he would say when she picked up the phone, so he created scenarios and hypothetical conversations, but in every practice, he clammed up, tongue-tied even in his mind, feeling inept. He wrote down some questions he might try.

Finally, one late evening before going to bed, he decided to chance another humiliation for him and pain for her. He'd call her in the morning and simply say, "Hello, Bev, this is Whit Coombs. How are you?"

But that night he suffered another nightmare, the intervals between them growing shorter—Hope's cancer-wracked body contorted, her corpse spewing hatred again, the familiar words of pure loathing stabbing him with fresh remorse and guilt and pain. He woke up weeping. Barney came to him and licked his face and whined and finally flopped down at Whit's side and placed his big head on his master's chest and sighed and settled.

Whit draped an arm over his dog. There was some comfort there, and he was grateful for it. The wind whistled outside and made the warm cabin seem even cozier than usual, contrasted with the brumal weather. But the wind made Whit feel even worse, lonelier, bereft of the one woman he had loved in his life, now gone, leaving him with epithets and enmity drilling into his heart and mind. He remained awake in his shame for the rest of the night.

In the morning he rolled out of bed and onto his knees on the rug beside his bed and prayed, "Lord Jesus, forgive me, a miserable sinner." When he finished, Whit remained on his knees, dropping his head onto the bed, wearied from the fresh nightmare. After a few moments, he rose to his feet and got on with his day.

He made his bed and let Barney out. Then he took out his heavy iron frying pan and began cooking eggs in abundant butter, sliding the eggs to one side as they congealed, then adding sausage patties. He cooked a block of frozen hash browns in the microwave, popped open a package of biscuits and set them to cook in the oven. While that food heated up, he made a pot of coffee. He let Barney in.

After breakfast and cleanup, he left his dog on the love seat and drove into Hastings Corners in the fresh sunlight, speeding along on the steaming black ribbon of road, snow piled up like white piping on the shoulders. He pulled up at Homer's Gas & Grocery. Inside, he waited for Homer to finish ringing up an old couple bundled against the winter weather despite the shining sun and melting snow glistening wetly on rooftops and highways.

"What can I do ya for?" Homer asked as the elderly customers left. He leaned on the counter in front of him, his chubby hands folded on a bare place between displays of beef jerky and zodiac keychains.

"Okay if I borrow your phone for a minute?"

"Sure, Whit. You don't need to ask, remember?"

"I don't want to take your kindness for granted."

Homer smiled. "Go ahead. My phone is your phone."

Whit edged around the counter and squeezed into Homer's tiny office and fished out Bev's card from his flannel shirt pocket. He punched in the numbers on the touch-tone telephone and waited, taking out the sheet of paper from his hip pocket and spreading it out on the cluttered desk to review his suitable questions.

The phone rang once, twice, and he nearly hung up, hoping she wasn't home because he was going to be clumsy again and say nothing or say too much or the wrong thing and hurt her feelings or just convince her that he was dimwitted and thought there was something wrong with her because of what happened with Merrone and Butz and he didn't want to talk about it with her at the Oktoberfest. She picked up.

Whit momentarily froze.

"Hello? Who is this?" she asked, her voice sliding from friendly to wary in the silence.

"Whit C-Coombs."

Bev's voice flipped back to friendly. Warm and friendly. "Oh, hello, Whit! Nice of you to call. How are you doing?"

"Um, how are you doing?"

"That's my question," she said, a small bell of laughter at the edge of her voice.

"Sorry. I mean, would you like to have another date, a real date? Like dinner?"

"How nice of you to ask. I thought you'd forgotten all about me. When might this be?"

"What day is today?"

"Today is Thursday, Whit."

"Saturday then?"

"I have a show in Morganton this Saturday, and a panel after that, then a judging for a high school competition. How 'bout the Saturday after this one?"

Whit had not anticipated so many questions. He paused, looked at his notes. She waited. Then he said, "Okay. How 'bout I pick you up at seven. Or would eight be better?"

"Six would be even better. I retire early at my age."

"Okay," he said, his mind scrambled with success. "I'll pick you up, then, at six, in nine days. Where do you live?"

"Do you still have my card? The one with my phone number and address written on the back?"

"Oh, got it. Dumb me. Okay, so where would you like to go? I don't know of any good restaurants, really. Church's Chicken isn't too bad."

"Let me surprise you," she said. He noticed how nice her voice was, and he suddenly felt elation.

"Okay, goodbye, Bev," he said, and hung up before she could respond.

"Stud," Homer said, and winked as Whit left the store after thanking him for the use of his phone.

Nine days later, in slacks and his blue sweater and a light down jacket, Whit climbed up the stairs to her garage apartment and knocked on her door. There were no lights on. And no response to his knocking. He tried again, and a third time.

She opened the door.

"You've been crying," he said, alarmed. "What's wrong?"

"Me, that's what's wrong. Whit, I just can't do this. I am so sorry," she said. Then she said, "I'm a mess" and turned away, rubbing her palms against her eyes, where her makeup had smeared.

"Is it something I said, or. . . "

She turned back to him. "You are a good man, Whit, but I can't go out with you. Or anyone," she said. "So if you'll continue to be kind, and accept what I've said, I'll just say I am so sorry, and let it go at that. Please leave me alone."

Beverly forced a sad smile and slowly closed the door.

It began to snow a bit, little puffs of pillow stuffing barely heavy enough to fall drifting back and forth and up a little on their way to the ground.

Whit stood silently in front of Beverly's door, thinking she might change her mind and open the door and go out with him. But she did not do any of those things, so he trudged down the stairs to his pickup truck and drove home in the growing storm.

CHAPTER 21

"If you want to control someone,
all you have to do is make them feel afraid."
—Paulo Coelho

AND SO THE WINTER CONTINUED, deeper, colder, one snowfall
after another descending before the previous storm could melt away,
drifts piling up like neglected responsibilities. Hanging over Whit like
a dangling dead branch, the coming trial of Buford Butz and Hacker
Merrone kept an edge on his attention.

The trial drew Beverly's attention as well. Word gets around in a small
mountain village, and one day as the trial was looming up, DA Calvin
Rider showed up at Beverly's apartment.

"I heard about your run-in with Mister Merrone and Mister Butz at
the Oktoberfest," he said after introducing himself.

Beverly stepped outside and pulled her door shut, folding her arms
in front of her in the cold air. "I'll bet you did," she said.

"As you know, I'm sure, I'm prosecuting the cases against Mister
Merrone and Mister Butz, and my only witness to the alleged murder is

Mister Coombs. Now, while I think he is a stalwart gentleman and that he is telling the truth, my case might be made stronger if you could share what it was that alienated you from the two defendants."

"That's private, Mister Rider."

"I'm sure it is, but if you would kindly come forward and provide testimony against their character, the chances of a conviction might improve. They're not all that strong now, to be perfectly candid."

A brisk wind kicked up, and Beverly hunched her shoulders against the sudden, penetrating chill.

"Perhaps we should go inside, Miz Andreeson. You look very cold," Rider said.

"No. I am sorry, sir. I appreciate the task before you. But I can't help you. Good luck with your prosecution."

With that, Beverly stepped back inside, shut the door, and made herself a cup of hot lavender chamomile tea to help with her shivering. The horror of testifying in a courtroom about her suffering at the hands of the two men made her tremble more than the winter wind.

Three days later, she suspended work on a painting in order to drive into Woodrow and advocate for a one-woman show in the coming spring at the Mitchum County Fine Arts Society. Every year a regional artist would be featured and allowed to hang their work in the small Fine Arts Center gallery for two months, and the society's board of trustees had encouraged Beverly to interview and apply. That opportunity was today at the board's monthly meeting.

She looked forward to confirmation. With their invitation in hand, she could begin to produce more work for display at the festival. She had plenty of fresh ideas to bring to canvas. It was an opportunity she had coveted. Bev knew from artist friends who had previously been honored that the board's invitation typically led to selection.

As she approached the small, stone Fine Arts Center building, she saw that all six of the parking places in front were taken, so she was forced to drive around back and park there. She found a spot between two Mercedes sedans. Trustees.

She parked and cut off her engine, noticing that a pickup truck had pulled crosswise behind her, effectively blocking her. Her pulse pounded as she emerged from her Honda and turned around. That's when the man loomed up.

She started to turn away, to run, but he was on her, jerking her around and shoving her back against her Honda. He was huge with a bushy beard, and as she began to panic, her heart thrumming fast in her chest, Beverly wondered how someone that big could be so quick.

His enormous, thick hands gripped her wrists and pushed her hands up and away from her body, pinning her, forcing her to fight for breath through the pain. While one of his hands squeezed her wrists together, the other came up with a piece of gray duct tape that he forced over her mouth, bruising her lips. He pressed his bloated, fetid body against her and ground his hips against hers. She could feel him through his filthy overalls as he panted through tobacco-stained teeth, his sour breath bathing her face in damp gasps. Bits of food were sprinkled in his gray-flecked beard.

"You been talkin' to that sumbitch Hoot Rider, girl, and you oughta know not one word from you needs be spoke in court 'bout that enjoyment my friends had with you a while back. You was drinkin' and wearin' something real enticin' and when they axed you to dance, you flipped 'em off. Bad move, teaser. You got what was comin' to ya.

"Now, know this, whore. You squeak one word to the law about my boys, and you'll get some more of this," he said, grinding his pelvis against her. "And it won't be just one or two of us, bitch!"

She was whimpering now, her legs wobbly, her eyes wild. Horrified and helpless, Beverly prayed someone would come out and make this bear of a man stop. Call the police. Intervene. *God, anything!*

She threw up in her mouth, duct tape keeping the vomit in. Some came out of her nose. It stung. Her coughing was muffled.

Another violent thrust from the bearded man and a feral voice. "Got it?"

Beverly nodded up and down again and again as she dissolved there in the parking lot of the Fine Arts Center, leaning against her Honda. She wept. The big man laughed and shoved her, mocking her stained pants.

"And there ain't no place safe. Keep that in mind, Beverly darlin'. We know where you live. Now, you have a nice day," he said, his deep voice like something from a mine shaft. Then he spat on her, spun away, climbed into his pickup, and left.

No one saw.

Beverly, sobbing, pulled the tape from her mouth, spit and spit again, wiped her face. Then she fell into her Honda, scraping one of the luxury sedans as she backed up, and sped home, digging bloody fingernails into the tape residue that would not come off her face and lips.

CHAPTER 22

"The defendant wants to hide the truth because
he's generally guilty. The defense attorney's job
is to make sure the jury does not arrive at that truth."
—Alan Dershowitz

DISTRICT ATTORNEY CALVIN "HOOT" RIDER briefed Whit
on how to testify when called to the witness stand, although Whit had
determined he would just tell the truth in recounting what he saw and
heard that night.

A boisterous crowd already filled the seats in the Ransom County
Courthouse when Whit arrived. To them, the trial was an event to ease
the boredom of a long winter, to provide entertainment and fuel for
arguments that would take the citizens into springtime and beyond. A
few leftover people stood in the back, and Whit had to push his way
through them to reach his seat.

The *Asheville Citizen-Times*, *Morganton News-Herald*, and *Charlotte
Observer* all covered the trial. Reporters were sprinkled throughout the
courtroom.

One big good old boy hissed, "There's that loony hermit!" and multiple remarks erupted around Whit, who held his head high.

"Leave him alone!" a young woman shouted. "He doin' the right thang!"

The remarks energized the background buzz as Whit moved down the aisle to Calvin Rider's table, glancing through the crowd unsuccessfully, hoping to spot Beverly. Her absence troubled him—set afire unease in his stomach not there before.

Whit took his seat next to the DA. Across the aisle, Hacker Merrone and Buford Butz were seated with Joel Huff, the public defender. All three men wore suits, white shirts, and ties. Butz and Merrone were clean shaven, their hair combed. It was difficult to recognize them at first, but then Whit spotted their eyes and the smug grins on their faces, and he knew them.

After a few whispered remarks from Calvin Rider to Whit, comments meant to encourage and provide optimism, the trial began. Opening statements surprised no one. Calvin Rider went first with a brief attempt at confidence, which failed. Joel Huff followed, brimming with goodwill and certainty. The opening statements concluded, and the trial moved on with the prosecution going first.

As the only witness for the prosecution, Whit was called immediately.

He related in short, terse sentences what he had seen that night. Rider worked hard to establish Whit's credibility—his service to country and the medals he had earned over the years, his courage in coming forward, his never having been charged with a major crime. Then he sat down and Huff rose, smiling, to cross-examine Whit.

Joel Huff began asking him questions, making it a point to speak toward Whit's right ear as much as possible. Whit had to ask the attorney to repeat himself in order to hear and understand the question, and quickly recognized the tactic. Whit countered by turning his left ear toward Huff, but that also reinforced his hearing deficit. Whit thought it was a brilliant but shameful manuever.

Other questions from Huff were anticipated: questions about Whit's vision, the stormy night making it hard to see, no corroborating witnesses. Huff's interactions with Whit were overly kind, almost condescending, as if Whit were damaged goods. His military service and disability were put on display, his reclusive lifestyle questioned. His recent violence toward the defendants came into play.

When Huff produced the blown-up photographs taken of Butz and Merrone after their confrontation at Whit's mailbox, the crowd gasped. Whit tried not to smile, forcing himself to maintain a neutral facial expression. Butz's broken, bloody nose and Merrone's cherry-tomato eye were powerful pieces of evidence to support Huff's claim that Whit had it out for the two mountain men and his testimony was just more of the same. When Calvin Rider later asked Whit what happened to provoke the injuries, scoffs from the defendants and dubious laughter from the gallery met Whit's explanation.

Then it was time for the defense. One witness after another, harvested from deep in the darkened hollers of the mountains, attested to the noble character and moral fiber of the defendants. Those with alibis for the men on the night of Tory Cook's murder were respectful, sober, and effusive in their praise of Hacker and Buford. The abundantly documented alibis held up, and when they weren't testifying, they could not suppress lofty attitudes and whispers and shared smiles.

Calvin Rider's brief cross-examination of the defense witnesses was flaccid, uninspired, and ineffective. The defense witnesses openly smirked at his questions.

There was never a question in Whit's mind as to the outcome of the trial. He had no illusions about justice being served. A hung jury was declared late that afternoon, and jubilation broke forth among the Merrone and Butz families and friends. The courtroom filled with cheers for the defendants who had just been set free, and curses and soft threats directed at Whit Coombs.

Whit worked his way through the reporters shoving their mics in his face as if he were fighting through clingy spiderwebs, pushing people and cell phone cameras aside. After brief conversations with Hoot Rider and Sheriff Della Render, he made his way outside and down the steps, searching for Beverly Andreeson.

He did not find her.

CHAPTER 23

"I don't even call it violence when it's in self-defense.
I call it intelligence."
—Malcolm X

THE DAY AFTER THE TRIAL was a Thursday, and Whit smiled when he saw Beverly's note card in the mailbox. He took it out and opened it, standing by the side of the road, hoping for good news—where she was, when he might see her again.

Instead, it read, *Dear Whit, I am far gone. When the verdict came down, I knew it would get worse for you, for me, and even if you take care of those two men, there will be others. They have friends. You can't protect me. Sheriff Render can't. I can't. Don't be lonely. Bev.*

Whit read the note twice, replaced it in the envelope, and walked slowly with Barney back to his cabin, the note in his hand.

Three nights after the hung-jury outcome, the defendants and three friends came for Whit in the middle of the night.

During the day, he kept his handgun on his person when he was outside. At night, he kept the gun and the speed loader at his bedside, trusting Barney to let him know if someone was coming.

Barney came through for him, nudging his big head against Whit's shoulder, a low whine coming from his throat. Whit awakened instantly, knowing.

The big dog jumped down as Whit slipped into jeans, a sweatshirt, and hiking boots. He donned his glasses. Gun in hand, he shoved the speed loader into his pocket and went to the front door where he heard the sound of engines. Headlights bathed the front of the house, followed quickly by a burst of fire from handguns, rifles, shotguns.

"Barney, *here!*" he shouted, pulling the big dog down on the floor with him as the windows blew in and slugs peppered the cabin. Whit scooted along the floor with his grip on the dog's collar. He shoved the dog into the bedroom with him, closing the door behind them, telling Barney to stay down. The gunfire stopped.

"Hey, tough guy!" It was Merrone. "You got no chance boy, none at all. I got four men with me, so you might as well come on out and face the music. Looks like your girlfriend, sweet Beverly, skedaddled. We'll get to her by and by, though. Come on out and we'll talk nice. If'n you don't, we'll kill you and your dog tonight. Might just burn down your shack with y'all in it. Or shoot you when you come runnin' out on fire."

Whit said nothing to the men, shaking his head. "This isn't fair," he muttered. The attack was as inept as Whit expected. Why hadn't they just ambushed him sometime? Set up an angled crossfire and waited? But now they had given him plenty of warning. *Still, even a halfwit with a handgun can be dangerous*, he thought.

"If you ain't gonna answer me, maybe you'll listen to this," Merrone shouted, and another volley of gunfire commenced.

Expecting at least one man to be at the rear of the cabin, Whit crouched and stepped quickly from the bedroom and out the back door, staying low, surprising the man waiting there with a rifle. Whit shot him in the forehead, and the man fell to the snow and did not move.

"Amateurs," Whit grunted.

As the fusillade from the front continued, Whit peeked around the corner of the cabin and saw four men firing away from behind their trucks, their gunfire masking the sound of their colleague's death. Whit fired twice at the largest of the shooters. The man slid to the ground, and when the others realized what happened, they turned their attention to Whit's position, dozens of bullets and buckshot raking the side of the cabin, chips of wood flying.

But Whit was already sprinting around to the other side, past the body bleeding in the snow, flanking the men firing from the trucks just as two sheriff's department cruisers roared onto the scene, sirens sounding, light bars flashing blue strobes across the white landscape.

The cruisers slid to a stop and their doors flew open. Officers took cover from gunfire as two of the attackers faced the newcomers and fired salvos in the direction of the cars, the bullets and buckshot plinking into the metal doors adding rapid-fire sounds to the night. And then the men fell—first one, cursing, then the other with a cry of anger. The night went silent.

Whit considered the number of dead and came up one short as he hunched down and slowly emerged from behind the cabin, eased through a stand of trees, and approached the trucks that had brought the shooters to his home. As he skirted the smaller of the trucks, the one he recognized as Merrone's, he came upon Buford Butz on the ground, his body pressed up against the wheel well, crying. There was blood all over his legs and one shoulder.

When Butz saw Whit, he said, "I been shot to pieces, Coombs, you sonuvabitch." Then he started to bring his shotgun up, his arms weak and wobbly, the gun suddenly heavy.

"No, don't!" Whit shouted.

Butz ignored the command, and as the shotgun continued rising to train on Whit, there was no other choice. Whit fired twice, the shotgun fell out of Butz's lifeless fingers, and the night became still again, the smell of gunpower and the small, drifting clouds of gunsmoke the only punctuation to the evening's agonies.

The ambush lasted less than ten minutes.

Whit heard a woman cry out. More adrenaline surged in his body.

He rushed forward, wending through the two dead men splayed out on the ground. He recognized Hacker Merrone. Another man, enormous with a bushy beard and wearing coveralls, was on his back, his face shot away, unrecognizable.

"Put your hands up! Now!" someone called from behind one of the patrol cars.

"It's me, Whit Coombs," he said, raising his hands.

"Drop the gun!" came the order. Whit recognized the speaker.

"It's me, Officer Hipp! Don't shoot. I'm putting my gun away," Whit said, bringing his arms down and tucking his gun into the back of his pants.

Hipp came out from behind his car and asked, "You okay, Coombs?"

"He's okay, but I'm not." It was Della, speaking from behind her car. The driver's side door, open for cover, was peppered with bullet and pellet holes. Her voice was weak, fluttery, shallow. Whit could not see her yet, but a clenching in his chest told him she had to be in serious trouble.

"You might put out 'Officer down' on the radio. I'm gonna need some help here," Sheriff Render called, her voice growing weaker. "Please."

Whit and Deputy Hipp raced to her side, the deputy shining his flashlight on the bloody woman, who'd propped herself up against the side of her cruiser. The tamped-down snow around her was dark with blood. Render passed out just as they reached her.

While Hipp tended to her bloody face even as he radioed for help, Whit tore open the uniform pants on the sheriff's left leg, exposing deep gunshot damage to her thigh, blood pumping out from a severed femoral artery. He reached inside her wound, nudging sticky muscle aside, and pinched shut the flow of blood.

"We can't wait for an ambulance!" Whit shouted.

"Agreed," Hipp replied. "You hold her and I'll drive. Officers Poteet and Belue will be here shortly. I'll fill them in about taking control of this mess, sealing it off."

"There's a dead shooter out behind the cabin."

"I'll tell 'em. Now, let's get the sheriff into the cruiser. You keep compression on the wound and I'll drive," Hipp said, his voice breathy. "Man oh man, will I drive."

And he did, the light bar flashing blue again, the siren a cry of anguish in the black night.

CHAPTER 24

"And I didn't realize what a kiss could be."
—Everly Brothers, "Til I Kissed You"

SHERIFF DELLA RENDER'S WOUNDS suffered at the shootout were grievous. She was airlifted to Asheville Regional Trauma Center. Her left femur was shattered in several places, and orthopedic surgeons took hours to reconfigure the bone pieces and stitch together the femoral artery. Tissue damage was horrific, with all four heads of her quadriceps shredded. Stray pellets from shotgun blasts had struck her face.

Whit drove back and forth to Asheville for days and sat and waited throughout Della's surgeries and treatment. Jimmy Fogel sat with Whit part of the time, praying off and on, his prayers fervent and specific and filled with praise while at the same time asking for skill for the surgical teams and peace for Render when the sheriff emerged from her sedation. And he prayed for Whit, for patience as he waited for Render to regain consciousness.

Whit never left her side other than to drive home quickly, change clothes, and take care of Barney, who had survived the attack unscathed.

As soon as the big dog had attended to his duties, Whit would hop back into his truck and speed to Della's bedside in Asheville, then Ransom.

While waiting for her to come out of her first surgery, Deputies Hipp and Poteet filled Whit in on the details in the aftermath of the attack. The man behind the cabin, as expected, was dead. So were Hacker and Buford and two other men, longtime confederates in a multitude of criminal activities. Borrowed forensics experts from the Asheville Police Department were busy figuring out the specifics of the ambush.

"But I'm afraid I have bad news on Sheriff Render," Deputy Hipp had said. He sat with Whit in the Asheville hospital canteen, both men sipping tepid coffee the morning after the shooting.

"Tell me."

Hipp turned and peered behind Whit. He said, "I'll tell you as soon as you relinquish possession of your revolver. I can't believe you're still packing, Mister Coombs. How the hell did you get in here with that?"

"I have no idea, but would you kindly fill me in on Della's wounds?" Whit asked, handing over his .38.

"I'm sorry to have to tell you this, but it looks like she's gonna lose sight in her left eye, and she ain't never gonna walk right again. Her leg was shot to pieces. Some damaged nerves in her face from shotgun pellets, might be kind of a droopy effect, like someone who's had a stroke. I'm sorry, Mister Coombs."

Whit just nodded. "Thank you, and thanks for hanging out here."

"She thinks highly of you, sir, and I think you respect her, too. Ain't no fun waitin', ever, but waitin' alone with no word is worse."

"So how did you manage to come to my rescue so fast? The attack had just started when y'all showed up. I'm grateful," Whit said.

"Sheriff's got a kid on the inside of Merrone's bunch. Good source of information," Deputy Hipp said. "But I'm not so sure you needed any help. You were doin' just fine when we showed up."

"Those guys weren't professionals," Whit said.

"Nope," Hipp said with a smile.

The doctors would not let Whit sit with Della Render in recovery, and only after Deputy Hipp leveraged his authority and made Whit a deputized officer was he allowed to see her. He waited with her there, and when she awoke, he took her hand and held it for a long time before they spoke. He tried not to stare at her left eye. It did not look damaged, but there were stitches nearby.

Her first words to Whit were, "How many were there, Whit?"

"Five, all dead."

"My officers?"

"All fine."

She smiled a different smile. "Better shots."

"Deputy Hipp saved your life. You were bleeding to death and he drove like hell to get you to the ER in time."

"Good man. He didn't say. I put him in command of the department for now."

"How are you doing?"

She knew. Somehow she knew.

"I'll be fine, Whit, but I'm not gonna be much to look at," she whispered, her voice hoarse. He gave her some ice chips. A small sob escaped from deep within her. He placed pressure in her palm and she squeezed back, tears falling.

"Yes, you will be fine." He wiped the tears away with a tissue.

"But I'll be different." The two of them were quiet for a while. "I need to sleep now, Whit. So tired. Will you be here when I wake up?"

"Yes."

"Good," she said, her smile off just a bit.

When she woke up three hours later, she turned her head and looked at Whit and put out her hand. He took it and kissed it, and something in his heart began to collapse.

"That was so nice, Whit. You are so kind."

He kissed her lips and his collapse was complete. She sighed and smiled that new smile again.

"I guess I won't be pulling a Rooster Cogburn, will I?"

"We'll see. You are being covered in prayer, Della. We'll see."

She fell asleep again.

Whit drove home quickly and aired Barney, grateful that Deputy Poteet had taken on the responsibilities for his boss's cat, Rex.

The next day, Whit waited outside her room while a nurse bathed her. After that, he surprised Della with a small basket with several gifts inside—a gift card to a pizza place, a get-well card with a kitten on it, and a thin package covered over by white copy paper that she withdrew and scrutinized.

"What's this?" she asked.

"Seeds."

"What kind?"

"They're *Rudbeckia hirta*. In plain English, black-eyed Susans."

She smiled again and reached out and took Whit's hand and brought it to her lips and kissed it.

In the ensuing days, Sheriff Render was finally allowed to go home, where a pleasant, efficient, and good-natured home health-care nurse supported her recovery. Della learned that she would always have a significant limp, and that her left leg would be a little bit shorter than her right leg.

After careful thought, analysis of her benefit package, and prayer, she decided to take early retirement with disability.

Whit Coombs came to see her every day, visiting her at her bungalow, making friends with Rex, and taking Della out and about to prevent cabin fever. They kissed often. The stitches in her face were removed.

One night, when she had specifically asked him to not come see her, Barney alerted Whit that someone was approaching the cabin. He reached for his revolver—finally returned to him from the forensics people—and strode out the front door with his friend at his side.

He did not recognize the car, which made him apprehensive. There had been vague threats from friends of Merrone and Butz and family members of the other men killed in the gun battle, but they had fizzled. Word had gotten out about Whit's handiness with a handgun.

It was dark, and after the car came to a stop and the headlights flicked off, he recognized Della Render as she emerged. He tucked his revolver away. She hobbled with her cane in one hand and a flat box in the other. Barney ran to greet her, tail wagging, and she told him he was a handsome boy.

Whit started to go to her but she said, "No, wait for me on the porch. I need the exercise. I want to come to you."

She was puffing a little when she reached his front door, where she handed him the pizza and said, "I know you like to keep to yourself. Understand that I like to keep to myself, too. But I was wondering if maybe we could keep to ourselves, maybe, um, together?"

Whit put his arm around Della, opened the door, and let her in.

EPILOGUE

"Mysteries of attraction could not always be explained
through logic. Sometimes the fracturing in two separate
souls became the very hinges that held them together."
—Lisa Kleypas, *Devil in Winter*

THE CEREMONY TOOK PLACE in the spring at God's Grace
Church, Jimmy Fogel officiating. Homer of Homer's Gas & Grocery was
best man, and relished the honor. Deputies Hipp and Poteet were honored
guests. Those six were the only people present.

Della Render Coombs did not lose her left eye. Her vision returned
and she claimed a miracle. Scattered across her face like a handful of faint
freckles, scars provided mute testimony to her injuries.

She sold her bungalow and moved in with her husband at the cabin
by the blue lake in the mountains. Barney was introduced to Rex, who
taught Barney his manners. They soon became friends.

The black-eyed Susans were planted in fresh soil in the spring.

Beverly Andreeson effectively disappeared. She was never seen again in those parts, but her paintings appeared now and then in cities in the northeast, recognizable by her captivating and profound use of grays and blacks.

Whit Coombs never had another nightmare.

ACKNOWLEDGMENTS

A LOT OF PEOPLE got behind me as I lumbered toward the completion of *Keeping to Himself*. I'd like to thank the professionals at Koehler Books, and that means John Koehler, Hannah Woodlan and her keen attention to detail, and Skyler Kratofil of the great cover designs. These folks are not only tops at their game, they are also fun. Tough to beat that. And special thanks to my book concierge, Rowe Carenen, who told me about Koehler Books and encouraged me to check them out. Wow! Thanks, Rowe.

I'd also like to acknowledge Jeff Phillips—the finest attorney in the Upstate, according to John Grisham (and Jeff)—who helped me with legal questions. And encouragement. And thanks to Tim Udouj and Joe Dentici, who encouraged me over an outdoor lunch (that they paid for) one lovely afternoon in picturesque Travelers Rest.

Our critique group, The Write Minds, was a tremendous source of constructive criticism and encouragement, particularly John Eells, Ken Crisp, Maxine Bennett, Melinda Walker, Dave Horner, Shannon Greene, James Raff, Marcia Pugh, and Katrina Kimbril. Also, thank you to old friend Byron Matthews III, who provided a key phrase for Whit Coombs' theology.

I'd like to thank Clay Stafford, Killer Nashville's founder and driving force, for his encouragement to keep writing a while back when I was seriously considering giving it up and moving on to something else—maybe beekeeping. And David Morrell, great encourager, who will never know what it meant to me to see him again after all those years.

And a thank you to my eldest daughter, Caitlin Carenen, for her steady encouragement.

CPSIA information can be obtained
at www.ICGtesting.com
Printed in the USA
BVHW081147250621
610447BV00004B/518

9 781646 633968